PRAISE FOR

ALL THE WRONG MOVES

"A 21-gun salute for *All the Wrong Moves*, a fast-paced, original, authentic military mystery that builds to a pulse-pounding finale."

—Carolyn Hart,
Pulitzer Prize–nominated author of the bestselling
Death on Demand series

"*All the Wrong Moves* has all the right stuff . . . Fast-paced adventure starring an irreverent heroine you'll never forget. I couldn't put it down!"

—Vicki Lewis Thompson,
New York Times bestselling author

"Samantha is great—sassy and indomitable and believable . . . [The] action never stops."

—Joanna Carl,
author of the bestselling Chocoholic Mysteries

"Merline Lovelace once again affirms her position as a five-star author with this strong look at military testing inside a wonderfully drawn investigative thriller."

—*Genre Go Round Reviews*

"What fun! Merline Lovelace delivers a wisecracking heroine with a fascinating and interesting occupation that teams her with a cast of eccentric and peculiar characters. If you are looking for a good laugh with a strong mystery, *All the Wrong Moves* is the perfect choice."

—*Fresh Fiction*

continued . . .

Berkley Prime Crime titles by Merline Lovelace

ALL THE WRONG MOVES
NOW YOU SEE HER

NOW YOU SEE HER

MERLINE LOVELACE

BERKLEY PRIME CRIME, NEW YORK

THE BERKLEY PUBLISHING GROUP
Published by the Penguin Group
Penguin Group (USA) Inc.
375 Hudson Street, New York, New York 10014, USA

Penguin Group (Canada), 90 Eglinton Avenue East, Suite 700, Toronto, Ontario M4P 2Y3, Canada
(a division of Pearson Penguin Canada Inc.)
Penguin Books Ltd., 80 Strand, London WC2R 0RL, England
Penguin Group Ireland, 25 St. Stephen's Green, Dublin 2, Ireland (a division of Penguin Books Ltd.)
Penguin Group (Australia), 250 Camberwell Road, Camberwell, Victoria 3124, Australia
(a division of Pearson Australia Group Pty. Ltd.)
Penguin Books India Pvt. Ltd., 11 Community Centre, Panchsheel Park, New Delhi—110 017, India
Penguin Group (NZ), 67 Apollo Drive, Rosedale, North Shore 0632, New Zealand
(a division of Pearson New Zealand Ltd.)
Penguin Books (South Africa) (Pty.) Ltd., 24 Sturdee Avenue, Rosebank, Johannesburg 2196,
South Africa

Penguin Books Ltd., Registered Offices: 80 Strand, London WC2R 0RL, England

This is a work of fiction. Names, characters, places, and incidents either are the product of the author's imagination or are used fictitiously, and any resemblance to actual persons, living or dead, business establishments, events, or locales is entirely coincidental. The publisher does not have any control over and does not assume any responsibility for author or third-party websites or their content.

NOW YOU SEE HER

A Berkley Prime Crime Book / published by arrangement with the author

PRINTING HISTORY
Berkley Prime Crime mass-market edition / May 2010

Copyright © 2010 by Merline Lovelace.
Cover illustration by Michael Gibbs.
Cover design by Rita Frangie.
Interior text design by Kristin del Rosario.

ISBN: 978-0-425-23476-1

BERKLEY® PRIME CRIME
Berkley Prime Crime Books are published by The Berkley Publishing Group,
a division of Penguin Group (USA) Inc.,
375 Hudson Street, New York, New York 10014.
BERKLEY® PRIME CRIME and the PRIME CRIME logo are trademarks of Penguin Group (USA) Inc.

PRINTED IN THE UNITED STATES OF AMERICA

10 9 8 7 6 5 4 3 2 1

To the men and women serving our country
and the families who often sacrifice so much to support them.

With special thanks to:

Gerald Luedecking, Michigan police officer,
U.S. Army reservist, and CID Protective Services agent,
for sharing some of his incredible expertise.

My RomVets buds—
women who have served or are now serving—
who did their best to keep this AF vet straight
on Army ranks, MP procedures,
and investigative techniques.

And most especially Maggie Price,
my friend, fellow author, and former crime analyst
with the Oklahoma City Police Department.
When two devious minds like ours get together, watch out!

CHAPTER ONE

OKAY. I admit it. I was conducting a totally unauthorized test the bright February afternoon I got up close and personal with a stone-cold killer. My only excuse is that the gizmo submitted for my team's evaluation was too slick not to play with.

Wait! I have another excuse. I'm a second lieutenant in the United States Air Force. Everyone knows butter bars are all velocity and no compass heading. I suspect my boss would assert that's doubly true in my case. Sadly, I would have to agree with him. I tend to jump into things feetfirst. My brief, disastrous marriage to Charlie Numnutz Spade being a case in point.

But back to my close encounter with a killer. I had no inkling that particular life experience awaited me when my team crowded into my cubbyhole of an office that morning. If I had, I would never have glanced at, much less dug into, the cardboard carton Dennis O'Reilly deposited on my desk. Oblivious to my fate, I peered at the box's Bubble-Wrapped contents.

"What's this?"

"This, oh Goddess of Gadgets, is the NLOS system you wanted to add to our test schedule. It just arrived."

Goddess of Gadgets is one of the titles O'Reilly has bestowed on me, along with Widget Woman, Techno Diva, and several others that can't be repeated in mixed company.

I've come up with a few for him, too. Nerdo Supreme is probably the most accurate. The lenses in his black-framed glasses are an inch thick, and you can see his frizzy orange hair coming at you from a block away. But the man is an absolute wizard when it comes to deciphering and tinkering with lines of software code. Too much of a wizard according to some. Unauthorized tinkering is what landed him on my team.

What team, you ask? Our official designation is Future Systems Test Cadre—Three. FST-3, if you're into acronyms which everyone even remotely associated with the military seems to be. We're a tiny microbe in the vast, amorphous amoeba known as the Defense Advanced Research Projects Agency.

Don't let that fancy name fool you. DARPA itself conducts zero research. Instead, it doles out billions to universities and high-powered think tanks to explore new technologies that could improve or advance military operations. Over the years, DARPA fostered the technology that led to surveillance satellites, the Internet, stealth aircraft, laser-guided munitions, and night vision, to name just a few of its more notable projects. The agency does all this by employing super-brainiac military and civilian program managers who occupy nice, cushy, air-conditioned offices at our headquarters in Arlington, Virginia.

Then there's FST-3 and our two sister cadres. *Our* mission is to evaluate projects too small for direct oversight by the scientists at DARPA headquarters. Translation: we play around with gizmos and gadgets submitted by whacko inventors and mom-and-pop businesses hoping to snag some of those billions DARPA tosses out.

FST-1 tests items with potential for cold-weather application. They operate out of an igloo up in Alaska, somewhere north of the Arctic Circle. FST-2 wades through saw grass and battles alligators in the Florida Everglades. FST-3's charter is to evaluate projects suited for desert environments.

There's desert, and then there's desert. If you want the real thing, you should boogie on out to our home base at Fort Bliss, Texas. It's a sprawling Army post that eats up most of the area around El Paso, Texas. The Franklin Mountains dominate the skyline to the west of the base, shadowing the muddy trickle of the Rio Grande as it snakes its way across the border into Mexico. If you do decide to visit, though, I'd better warn you that blissful the post is *not*! At any given moment, soldiers are learning to fire things that go boom out our one-point-three million acres of test range.

Back to my little team. We call Fort Bliss home, but when we conduct our quarterly field evaluations, we bundle up ourselves and the projects we've selected for testing and deploy to a remote corner of those bazillion acres. That's what we were scheduled to do the very next morning . . . with the gizmo Dennis just plunked down on my desk.

"So that's the NLOS system," I said with a nonchalance that fooled no one. "Er, what exactly do the initials stand for again?"

"Non . . . line . . . of . . . sight," O'Reilly spelled out with exaggerated pity for my non-techie brain.

His barely veiled sarcasm didn't surprise me any more than my need for a memory jogger surprised him and the others who'd trooped into my office. We've worked side by side for almost a year now. I know their foibles and they know mine. Together we add up to a lot of foibles.

Guess I'd better introduce you to the whole team. There are five of us assigned—or condemned, depending on your point of view—to FST-3. Three civilians in the persons of O'Reilly; Dr. Brian "Rocky" Balboa, our test engineer; and Dr. Penelope England. Pen earned a doctorate in two different bioenvironmental specialties and is so-far-out-there brilliant she has trouble communicating with mere mortals. Which might give you a clue how she ended up on FST-3.

I represent the military side of the house, along with Staff Sergeant Noel Cassidy, a muscled-up Special Ops type working through some sexual identity issues. Don't ask!

I won't bore you with every painful detail of how I, Samantha JoEllen Spade, product of a long line of boozers and losers, came to be in charge of this motley crew. Suffice to say that after catching my jerk of an ex-husband doing the dirty with our bimbo of an ex-neighbor, I decided I needed a change of scene. So on the advice of a really hot pilot stationed at Nellis AFB, right outside Vegas, I quit my job as a cocktail waitress at the Paris casino, tucked my bachelor's degree in Management from UNLV under my arm, and sauntered into an Air Force recruiter's office.

Big mistake. Huge. Some people are just not cut out for rules and regulations.

Although . . .

To be fair, it's not entirely the Air Force's fault we're such a bad match. I've never done real well at taking orders. Just ask my mother. She'll tell you I also have something of a mouth on me. Combine those traits with my aforementioned tendency to dive into things and you can guess why my supervisor at the Air Force Research Lab "loaned" me to DARPA. And why my supervisor at DARPA takes several hours, sometimes days, to work up his courage before he returns my calls.

Most of the time I shake my head and wonder how the heck I'm going to make it through my four-year commitment without ending up in front of a firing squad. At odd moments, though, this really strange sensation sneaks up on me. Like when I stop at a fast-food joint and/or gas station and folks glance over at my boots and ABUs.

Ooops, there's that initial thing again. Sorry. ABU stands for airman battle uniform. They're the Air Force's latest version of haute couture. Baggy pants; boxy big shirt; and a brimmed, peaky patrol cap, all done in pixelated brown, green, tan, and blue tiger stripes. Said stripes are imprinted on a fabric specially treated to reduce the wearer's heat signature.

Wish I could tell you that reduction thing works on the inside as well as it does on the outside. I may not give off much of a signature externally. Come summer, though, all it takes is five or ten minutes in the high desert heat to leave me gasping for breath and my dark red hair a sweaty tangle inside my patrol cap.

Sweaty or not, I'm always surprised by the reaction of civilians I encounter off-post. The respect in their eyes isn't for me, God knows, but for what these combat boots and baggy fatigues represent. Gives me a goosey feeling to think I am now a walking embodiment of centuries of honor and tradition and service to one's country.

I get even goosier when I think my little team might stumble across an idea or invention that could make said service easier on the troops out there actually doing it. That faint hope was swimming around somewhere at the back of my mind as I poked at the Bubble-Wrapped contents of the carton O'Reilly had deposited on my desk.

"So this is the non . . . line . . . of . . . sight system," I commented, treating him to a taste of his own sarcasm.

Actually, now that he'd jogged my memory I remembered reading the specifications for a pair of souped-up video goggles. The inventor claimed they could see over hills, around buildings, and through trees. Curious to examine this marvel, I peeled back the layers of plastic wrap.

I've learned the hard way to handle items submitted to my team for evaluation with extreme caution. I'm still sporting a patch of red, irritated skin from an inflatable communications armband that ballooned up and refused to un-balloon.

Thus my wariness as I lifted out and unwrapped what looked like a pair of futuristic shades. I scoped them out from all angles and decided these babies looked *très* cool. Tubular-shaped and less than an inch wide, they sported a narrow slit running horizontally along the center. Presumably to let the wearer see out and allow the transmitted images in.

They had a sexy sort of sci-fi allure. When I slipped the specs on, I got the feeling that I'd morphed into Terminator Woman. All I needed to complete the image was a lipstick red bodysuit and a sawed-off shotgun tucked into a holster on my hip.

Angling my chin, I squinted through the slit while our test engineer lifted out what looked like an ordinary egg carton. Inside the carton were a dozen round, shiny disks nested in cardboard cups.

"Battery operated sensors," Rocky commented.

In direct contrast with the he-man nickname we've bestowed on him, Dr. Brian Balboa is as far from the Rocky Balboa of movie fame as you can get. He used to work at DARPA headquarters. None of us know the precise reason he left. We suspect it might be due to his unfortunate tendency to expel gas when he gets too excited. He's also let drop one or two cryptic comments about a former colleague whose eyebrows have yet to grow back. Whatever the reason behind his assignment to FST-3, Rocky really gets off on this ultra-high-tech stuff. An almost ecstatic expression came over his face as he turned one of the shiny disks over in his palm and stroked its wire tail.

"This is an omnidirectional transmitter. The inventor claims it can backscatter sun- and moonlight off aerosols in the atmosphere."

I didn't even try to hide my ignorance this time. "Ooooo-kay."

"The air around us contains a significant amount of atmospheric particles," he explained earnestly. "That's especially true during daylight, where you encounter minimal solar interference at solar-blind wavelengths."

I exchanged looks with Staff Sergeant Cassidy. Noel didn't exactly roll his eyes, but he darn came close. With more than twelve years in Special Ops under his belt, he's counting the days until his shrink clears him to get back to the world of camouflage face paint and midnight insertions into hostile areas. In the meantime, he is stuck with us.

Thankfully, Pen stepped into the breach. "Think of the particles as tiny mirrors," she translated.

None of O'Reilly's sarcasm there. Dr. Penelope England is nothing if not serious. About everything. I've tried to lighten her up. Trust me, this is *not* an easy task. The woman's idea of a really fun weekend is strapping on her Birkenstocks and attending a Scientists Against Biospheric Exploitation rally.

"Sound waves travel in a direct line," Pen explained, tucking a wayward strand of salt-and-pepper hair into her lopsided bun. "So do radio and optical signals. That's why we position relay towers atop hills or tall buildings, above potential obstacles. The towers have to be in the line of sight to receive and redirect the waves."

"It's also why you have to stand close to a video game console like the Wii for the controls to work," O'Reilly put in. "Optical signals become distorted if they have to travel too far."

I may be a little slow on the uptake but stuff sinks in eventually.

"So if you scatter tiny 'mirrors' to catch waves refracted off atmospheric particles," I said slowly, "the signals don't have to travel as far . . . or follow a straight line."

"Exactly!"

Pen beamed like someone who's just taught her pet orangutan to sit up and sing. Or chirp. Or emit whatever musical sounds orangutans make.

Thinking hard, I took off the goggles and turned them

over in my hand. If these suckers performed as advertised, they might fit into DARPA's Urban Leader Tactical Response, Awareness, and Visualization Initiative. The goal of the initiative was to give squad leaders engaged in door-to-door operations the ability to assess the situation and communicate with his or her troops using nonverbal, digitally recognized signals.

The project was huge. One of those monster programs I mentioned before that could rain megabucks down on individuals or firms invited to participate at the next level. More to the point, the project was being personally honcho'ed by my boss, Dr. David Jessup.

As I mentioned earlier, Dr. J and I have a somewhat precarious relationship. Do you blame me for wondering if these slick little goggles could create a bond? Or for adding the NLOS system to our already crammed test schedule?

"Is the van already packed?"

"It is," Sergeant Cassidy confirmed. "I moved it to the secure lot an hour ago, but I can drive over and add this to the inventory of test items."

"That's okay. I'll take the system home with me tonight. I want to read the specs again and make sure I understand them before we head out to Dry Springs."

My intentions at that moment were completely honorable. I swear! I was even feeling a sense of noble dedication as I toted the carton out to my car after we agreed to reconvene at oh-dark-thirty the following morning to depart for our test site.

Such lofty matters as dedication to duty and contributing to the advancement of military technology couldn't compete with the emotions that gripped me when I approached my new car, however. Sheer delight topped the list.

The beat-up Bronco I'd taken in exchange for a quickie divorce was no more. Thanks to the Fort Bliss Credit Union and the rogue FBI agent who'd blown up the Bronco several months ago, I now tooled around in a sleek little Sebring convertible. The Sebring probably isn't the wisest choice of vehicles for someone with a heavy foot, but what the heck. It's a loooooong ride out to our test site, with mile upon mile of empty road. Besides which, I make it a point to pay every speeding ticket promptly. They know me out there in Nowhere, Texas, and I'm not about to lose my license or worse, spend the night in a one-cell lockup with the local drunk. Those fines make a serious dent in my discretionary spending at the end of the month, but a girl's gotta have some fun.

The convertible still retained enough of that sensuous new car smell to elicit a sigh of pure joy as I buckled in. That delicious scent and the feel of the late afternoon sun on my face as I left the parking lot were almost enough to make me forget the ridiculous twenty-five-mile-per-hour speed limit on post.

As mentioned, Fort Bliss is a humongous Army training center. I should also mention that the oldest part of the post sprang up during the Indian Wars. It hasn't changed all that much since. I bring my team's cramped facilities and outmoded HVAC system to the attention of the deputy post commander on a regular basis. He doesn't return my calls anymore, either.

That negative input aside, I have to confess a fascination for the post's history. The Fort Bliss museum gives glimpses into military life back before ABUs and MREs. Sorry. That's meals ready to eat.

On a more personal level, there's a definite plus to working on a monster training base. It's crammed with troops. Hundreds of troops. Thousands of troops. All shapes, sizes, and ranks. Terrific pickings for a relatively recent divorcée with legs that used to earn some great tips back in my cocktail waitress days.

My legs don't exactly show to advantage in baggy ABUs, but I *have* managed to dip into this vast testosterone pool a time or two. I also enjoyed a brief but satisfyingly torrid liaison with an instructor at the Avenger Missile School on post before I hooked up with Border Patrol Agent Jeff Mitchell.

Mitch and I have been seeing each other for several months now, and if he hadn't called to say he was running a little late for our rendezvous at our favorite pizza joint that evening, I might never have taken the nonline of sight optical sensor system for a spin.

But he was. So I did.

In my defense, the components were just sitting there in their nest of Bubble Wrap. The narrow, tubular glasses. The egg carton full of disks. The detailed description of how to activate the sensors and receive transmissions. I couldn't leave them in the front seat of an open convertible while I waited for Mitch inside Perry's Pizza Parlor, could I?

Don't ask why I didn't lock the carton in the Sebring's trunk and go my merry way. I've already asked myself that a dozen times. All I can say is that rather than wait in the noisy restaurant, I decided to sit in the sun and contemplate the stretch of desert across from the strip mall.

Although I would have rather parked overlooking, say, a stretch of Big Sur, I will admit the desert has a beauty all its own. The low, slanting sun had painted the earth in twenty-seven shades of red and brown. Off in the distance, the Franklin Mountains poked their rugged peaks into a near cloudless sky.

It was the wide-open vista between me and the mountains that got me thinking. All that empty space looked very similar to the remote site my team and I would deploy to first thing in the morning. Only a few twisted mesquite, some spiny cacti, and the gaping slash of an arroyo to add character to the landscape. Not a lot of obstacles out there to see over, around, and through.

Right behind me, on the other hand, were all kinds of obstacles. Twisting, I skimmed a glance along the E-shaped strip mall. The shops contained pretty much your usual assortment of businesses catering to the nearby military population. A dry cleaner. A Daylite Delite Donut shop. A health-food store for the physical fitness nuts like Sergeant Cassidy. A theater complex at one end, an

All-American Fitness Center at the other. Plenty of nice, solid structures to mess up optical waves.

I debated another few moments before giving in to irresistible impulse to take the system for a short run. Just for a few minutes, to see if it would even turn on. No one had to know 'cept me.

Emptying the egg carton, I stuffed the shiny round disks into various pockets. That's one major plus for ABUs. The shirt alone has four Velcro'ed flap pockets. Inside those are sewn-in pouches to hold small tools or flashlights or tubes of lip gloss. That's in addition to the pencil pocket on the left forearm. I once thought the pencil holder would be perfect for tubes of lip gloss, too. The gloss bubbled up in the desert heat, oozed through the cap, and ran down my arm. I had to toss my uniform shirt. Just thought you should be forewarned . . .

ABU pants also have flaps and pockets everywhere. As a result, I had more than enough storage capacity for the sensors, my car keys, ID, wallet, and cell phone. With my cap crammed over my hair and the goggles dangling from one hand I exited the Sebring.

The sensors clinked as I headed for the service drive between the dry cleaner and the donut shop. I placed two in the alleyway and a couple more behind the donut shop. Another fit nicely on the window ledge of a photography studio. I put one atop a Dumpster and decided that should be enough to play with.

Back in the parking lot, I flicked the switch to activate the goggles. According to the specs, the tiny transmitter embedded in one stem would send signals to the closest sensor. That disk would relay the signal to the next nearest sensor, and so on and so on. Reversing the process, each sensor would then bounce back imagery captured by their electronic eyes.

I stood there in my best Terminator Woman stance. Legs spread. Hands on hips. Head cocked expectantly.

Nothing happened. Zero. Nada. Zilch. All I could see through the slit was a thin slice of the parking lot. Disappointed, I was ready to retrieve the sensors when a small hum sounded in the right earpiece of the glasses. A second later, blotches of vivid color exploded onto the tiny, transparent screen.

"Whoa!"

I staggered back, bombarded by startling images. They chased across the narrow slit of a screen, so many and so fast I got dizzy. Only then did I remember I was supposed to turn my head in the direction of an individual sensor to focus on the imagery it was transmitting.

I angled around and breathed a sigh of relief when everything faded except a view of some banged-up garbage cans silhouetted against a brick wall. Took me a moment to assimilate the scene.

"Well, whaddya know."

Damned if I wasn't "seeing" through the sensor I'd left on the Dumpster around a corner!

Cautiously, I turned my head a few degrees to the right. The cans blurred and a view of the alleyway materialized. The scene was so clear I could read the stenciled warning above a gas main. Another few degrees and I picked up some birds perched on a telephone wire strung between the buildings.

Okay, this was too cool for words! Much more fun than most of the items submitted for our evaluation.

Moving cautiously, I walked forward a few yards. The images projected inside the narrow slit faded, blossomed, faded again. As long as I maintained a direct line of sight with one of the sensors, I could network to the others. Suddenly I stopped dead.

"What the . . . ?"

Frowning, I focused my full attention to the figure on the screen. The sensor on the photography studio's window ledge had picked him up. He was positioned next to a brick wall, half obscured by a white van.

The black ski mask covering his face sounded the first alarm inside my head, but it was the pistol he held in a two-fisted shooter's stance that set off loud, blaring Klaxons.

CHAPTER TWO

I stood rooted to the pavement. Was I really seeing what I thought I was? Was that a man crouched behind that van? Aiming a pistol?

My heart slamming against my ribs, I tried to force my disbelieving brain to confirm the image. When the terrifying reality hit home, I had two, maybe three seconds to react. I used one of them to whip off the glasses and spin around. My pounding heart almost jumped out of my chest when I spotted the white van not thirty yards behind me. From this angle, I couldn't see the shooter, but I knew he had a clear view of the health-food store and the fitness center next to it.

The very busy fitness center. With people entering and exiting. Some of them in uniform.

I didn't stop to think about the fact that I was totally

exposed there in the parking lot. Or that I might draw the shooter's fire. Waving both arms, I screeched a warning.

"He's got a gun! Take cover!"

The people in the vicinity did exactly what I would do in the same situation. They turned to see who the heck was shrieking at them.

In that frozen instant of time when they stood there, motionless, trying to grasp what was happening, the shooter fired. Crack. Crack. Crack. Three shots in quick succession. I heard one thud into something metallic, then the splinter of shattering glass.

Everyone was screaming now and throwing themselves to the pavement or sidewalk. I dived for the nearest car. A heavyset male in a blue jogging suit did the same. Crouched alongside a midnight blue Tahoe with an extended cab, he snatched a cell phone from his gym bag.

A movement just above him brought my glance whipping up. There was a woman in the driver's seat of the Tahoe, I saw in those seconds of sheer terror. She must have just pulled into a parking place because her SUV's engine was still idling.

The splintering glass I'd heard was her window. I could see her face through the jagged shards. Framed by a chin-length sweep of pale blond hair, her features were slack with shock and disbelief.

"Hey!" I screamed. "Get down!"

Why in God's name does *everyone* turn to the source of a shout? Instead of ducking, the woman slewed around and spotted me waving at her wildly. Then her stunned gaze zinged past me to the van. And the shooter! She must have caught a glimpse of him from her elevated position because her eyes went wide with recognition of imminent danger. A millisecond later he fired again.

Oh, God! She's hit.

That's all I could think as the woman jerked sideways and dropped out of sight. All I had *time* to think before the Tahoe lurched forward, revealing the jogging-suit guy who'd taken cover behind it. He dropped to the pavement and the heavy SUV rolled on, gathering speed.

The driver must have knocked the gearshift when she went down, I remember thinking in absolute terror. Kept her foot on the gas.

When her vehicle headed right for the people spread-eagle on the pavement, I abandoned my cover and lurched into a stooped-over run. Looking back, I'm not exactly sure what I intended to do. Sprint across the parking lot, I guess, wrench open the Tahoe's door, and yank on the steering wheel to keep it from rolling over those terrified gym patrons.

I'd taken only a couple of crablike strides when the SUV suddenly cut left. Tires screeching on the asphalt, it now aimed for the white van. I heard another shot, or thought I did. Then the Tahoe crashed into the van and shoved it forward a good five yards, exposing the shooter. He pumped out another frantic shot just before the Tahoe's rear end spun in a vicious arc.

The next few milliseconds seemed to play out in ultra-slow motion. The heavy SUV slammed into Ski Mask.

He crashed into the brick wall behind him. Bounced off. Dropped in a crumpled heap at the entrance to the alley.

I had started in that direction when the driver jammed her vehicle into reverse. She couldn't have seen the body lying directly behind and below her tailgate. She had to feel it, though, when her vehicle crunched over him.

I'm not ashamed to admit I felt only a swift sense of relief when I saw the Tahoe hump over the guy. Kind of hard to work up a lot of sympathy for someone who's taking potshots at you and everyone around you.

The Tahoe skidded to a stop, and I reached it a few seconds later. Exercising extreme caution, I edged around the front fender and spotted the gunman lying face-down. The black knit mask still covered his face but other, squishy parts of him were all too visible. The SUV must have crushed every bone in his chest.

That one glance was enough to tell me there wasn't anything I could do for him. It was patently obvious that he'd fired his last shot. Just to be safe, I aimed a swift kick at the weapon lying a few feet from his out-stretched arm. The semiautomatic clattered across the pavement, well beyond his reach, and I checked out the SUV's driver.

She sat hunched over the steering wheel. Her breath came in loud, shuddering gasps. Blood blossomed from cuts on her temple and cheek and ran down her neck, staining the collar of her uniform. Like me, she wore field dress but hers were Army BDUs instead of Air Force ABUs. Remind me to explain the difference sometime, when I'm not pumping pure fear and staring at a blood-spattered profile.

"Are you hit?"

She jumped and flashed me a terrified look. "The . . . ? The shooter?"

"It's okay," I said swiftly. "You nailed him."

Her gaze cut to the side-view mirror. Her breath rattled in. Out. In again.

"Is he dead?"

"From the looks of it. What about you? Did he hit you?"

"I'm . . . I'm okay."

"No, you're not. You've got glass embedded in your face. Don't touch it!" I warned as she put a trembling hand to her cheek.

I leaned in and searched for signs of a more serious injury amid the blood and glistening shards.

"The bullet that shattered the window?" I asked urgently. "It didn't hit you?"

"I . . . don't think . . . so."

My glance dropped to the patches on the front of her uniform blouse. They provided her name and rank, and the "MP" patch on her left arm gave a pretty good idea of where this woman had found the guts to career her vehicle across the parking lot and into the killer.

"Sit quiet, Sergeant Roth. The police and EMT are on their way."

Or so I hoped! Surely Jogger Guy had called 911. Just to make sure I plunged my hand into my shirt pocket and groped for my cell phone. I heard the wail of sirens at the same moment I dragged it out.

"Here comes the cavalry." I searched her face, my stomach clenching at the dead white pallor under rivulets of blood. "Hang in there, Roth."

"Stay with me," she whispered.

"I will. I promise."

"Thanks, Lieutenant."

She sagged against the seat back. Her eyes closed, then popped open again when my cell phone belted out a slightly raunchy rendition of "The Eyes of Texas." Sheer reflex had me pressing the answer button.

The phone is so crammed with features it takes an astronaut to operate it. FST-3 might be at the bottom of DARPA's food chain, but we *are* a component of a government agency charged with developing new technologies. That meant the slick little jobbie in my hand could do just about everything but scramble eggs. It would probably do that, too, if I could figure out all the buttons and menu choices.

At the moment, the best I could do was bring up an instant, astoundingly vivid image of the caller. The tanned face with the white squint lines at the corners of his eyes was one I knew well.

"Mitch! Where are you?"

"Almost to Perry's. Where are you?"

"In the parking lot outside Perry's. There's been a shooting."

"Christ! Are you okay?"

"Yeah, but the guy with the gun isn't."

Mitch clicked instantly into his law enforcement alter ego. I'd encountered it the first time when he and I were chasing that rogue ex-FBI agent I mentioned. The one who blew up my old Bronco. The bastard also torched my team's test lab out in the desert, by the way, then proceeded to drive Mitch and me off a cliff before a well-placed shot took him out. I wasn't real sorry to see him get dead, either.

"I can hear the sirens," Mitch rapped out. "Stay behind cover until they secure the scene."

I didn't tell him Sergeant Roth had already secured it. I didn't have time. Three vehicles careened into the parking lot at that moment. Two more followed mere moments later. Sirens wailing, strobe lights flashing, they cordoned off our end of the parking lot.

Heavily armed police officers exited the vehicles and took up defensive positions while they assessed the situation. The guy in the blue jogging suit jumped up and started to run toward them. One of the officers bellowed at him to stop, put his hands up, and keep them up.

Jogging-suit guy did as he was instructed. When the cops approached, he must have given them a quick recap of events because two officers immediately peeled away from the others and rushed over to the Tahoe. One radioed for an EMT team before he and his partner checked out the figure sprawled at the entrance to the alley. The younger of those two pulled on latex gloves and went down on a knee to check for a pulse. I don't know why I held my breath until he shook his head. It was pretty obvious even from where I stood Ski Mask was mush.

One of the cops stayed with the body. To preserve the crime scene, I guessed. The other came back to the Tahoe and questioned me while the EMTs worked on Sergeant Roth.

"I'm Officer Foster, El Paso PD." Producing the inevitable black notebook, the lanky young cop glanced at my name tag. "Could I have your full name, Lieutenant Spade?"

"Samantha JoEllen Spade."

"You assigned to Fort Bliss?"

"I'm assigned to a forward unit of the Defense Advanced Research Projects Agency. We're a tenant on Fort Bliss."

"Why don't you tell me exactly what happened?"

There it was. The question I'd been dreading. If I could have come up with an explanation of how I'd zeroed in on the shooter that didn't involve the NLOS system, I would have.

Unfortunately, I couldn't think that fast. My brain was still scrambled from the shooting. So I did a mental squirm and launched into what I intended as a layman's description of atmospheric backlight scatter and omnidirectional transmitters. I had the glasses in hand and was showing them to a very skeptical Officer Foster when a screech of tires on asphalt announced another arrival.

I turned in time to see Mitch leap out of his dusty gray pickup. He'd just come off shift and was still in his

Border Patrol greenies, with the usual fifteen pounds of lethal weaponry attached to his utility belt. He'd shed his floppy brimmed boonie hat, though, and there was just enough late afternoon sun left to bring out a glint of gold in his buzz-cut hair.

The first time I met Border Patrol Agent Jeff Mitchell I thought he looked a lot like my ex. Same broad shoulders, same impressive set of muscles under his greenies. The resemblance didn't win him any Brownie points at the time. Just goes to show you can't judge really hot studs by their appearance. Took me all of five or ten minutes to realize Mitch was as smart as he was buff. *Un*like my ex.

He was stopped at the cordon but flashed his ID, gestured to me, and was waved on. Naturally. It's a cop thing.

You think the military is a tight-knit community? True, we're all brothers and sisters in arms. But that's only when there are civilians in the vicinity. If it's just a bunch of uniforms hanging around a bar, our separate branches of service inevitably come into play. Then we're soldiers or sailors or marines or airmen or coasties.

Within those separate branches, the circles get even tighter. Army tank drivers hold themselves aloof from infantry grunts. Air Force fighter pilots may make noises about how we're all part of the same team and everyone's essential to the mission, but they can barely hold back a smirk when talking about trash haulers. (Their label, not mine, for transport pilots.) Even in

DARPA, which is predominantly civilian, you'll find a distinct pecking order.

I mention this because however tight we think we are in the military, we're loose as a goose compared to law enforcement types. The minute two or more cops get together, everyone else ends up on the outside looking in. That's exactly where I found myself, like, thirty seconds after Mitch assured himself I was still in one piece.

"That the shooter?" he asked Officer Foster.

"What's left of him."

"Mind if I take a look?"

Foster decided a Border Patrol agent would know his way around a crime scene and nodded. While he and Mitch went to inspect the body, I went to check on Sergeant Roth. She had exited her Tahoe and was sitting at the open back end of an ambulance. The EMT techs had picked the glass from her face and were cleaning the cuts.

Now that they'd swabbed away most of the blood I could see she was a few years older than me. Twenty-eight or -nine, I guessed, with her pale blond hair cut in a bob tapered high in back and slightly longer in front, so the ends just brushed her jaw. Some of her color had returned, and I was relieved to see the glazed look had left her amber eyes.

"How are you doing?"

I directed the question at the sergeant, but one of the EMT techs answered for her.

"She'll be okay. The safety glass they install in vehicles these days comes with a laminated liner. The glass breaks up into big chunks instead of the jagged shards that used to cause such deep lacerations. We'll transport her to the hospital once the police finish with her and let the docs give her a once-over."

"I don't need to go to the hospital," Roth countered.

"Let's see how you're doing after you talk to the investigators."

When the techs finished with their patient and gathered the tools of their trade, I sank down beside her.

"Might not hurt to let the docs check you out."

"I'm okay," she insisted and threw a grim look at Mitch and the others. "Who's the guy in Border Patrol greens?"

"His name is Jeff Mitchell. We were meeting at Perry's for dinner."

She forced her attention back to me. "I haven't thanked you, Lieutenant. When you shouted that warning . . ." She stopped and swallowed hard. "You saved my life."

"You saved a lot more. No telling how many people might have been killed or wounded if you hadn't taken such decisive action."

"Well, thanks anyway. My name's Diane, by the way. Diane Roth."

"Samantha Spade."

She held out her hand. I took it, noting that her grip was firm and sure. No limp fingered, girly-girl handshake for her. I'm still working on mine.

Officer Foster returned then. Mitch stood aside with

me while the patrolman took Roth's statement. The MP patch on her arm brought the cop thing into play immediately. Foster treated her with the courtesy one professional gives another. Especially after he elicited the fact that Roth had served in Afghanistan.

"What unit?"

"Five-forty-sixth MP Company, out of Fort Stewart."

"I was with the Seventy-second ANG in Iraq," Foster told her. "Rotated back to my civilian job last year."

"You guys saw some heavy action."

"Yeah, we did. So what's the story here? Where were you when the suspect started firing?"

"I'd just pulled into a parking space by the health food store. Annette, the woman who takes care of my kids when I'm on swings or mids, asked me to stop by on my way home and pick up this special brand of low-sodium tomato sauce she uses in her lasagna."

Frowning, Roth lifted a hand to her cheek while she related the details with a cop's precision.

"I was reaching for the keys to cut the ignition when I saw everyone hit the sidewalk. I guess I just froze, wondering what the hell was going on, because the engine was still running when my side window shattered. That's when I heard the lieutenant shout. I twisted around, saw her, and . . ."

She broke off and chewed on the inside of her lower lip for a moment or two. I did a little chewing myself. It's one thing to hear shots and react instinctively. Something else entirely to go through the whole terrifying sequence second by lethal second.

"I twisted around," Roth repeated in a low voice. "Saw the lieutenant. When I looked past her to the alleyway, I spotted the shooter at almost the same instant he fired again. I threw myself sideways on the seat, then just . . . just acted on instinct."

"Your Tahoe took several hits," Foster commented. "Do you think the guy was aiming at you?"

"Yes. Maybe. I'm not sure." Frowning, she sorted through the possibilities. "I was in my seat, elevated, a perfect target. Everyone else was flat on the ground or behind cover."

"Why didn't you just put metal to the pedal and drive away? Out of danger?"

"I wanted to! Believe me, that was my first inclination. But there were all those people . . ."

Foster nodded and made a few more notes. "That should do it for me. The homicide unit is on the way. The detectives will want to talk to both of you. They'll also probably need to impound your vehicle as evidence."

"Yeah, I figured." Roth seemed resigned to the loss of her wheels but gave her watch a worried glance. "I'm supposed to pick up my kids at six."

"Anyone you can call to handle that for you?" the patrolman asked.

My glance dropped to her left hand. No ring, I noticed, and understood why she worried her lower lip between her teeth again.

"I can try to reach my neighbor. But when she called to ask me to pick up the tomato sauce, she mentioned she was all the way across town at a meeting of the Red Hat Society."

"Before we do anything else," Officer Foster said with a nod toward the alleyway, "I need you and the lieutenant to take a look at the deceased. He doesn't have any identification on him. Maybe you can ID him."

Whoa! That brought me up short. I hadn't really reached the point of speculating on Ski Mask's identity yet. Subconsciously I'd sort of assumed this was just another random act of violence. The disturbed action of some psycho determined to leave his twisted mark on history.

Officer Foster's comment raised all sorts of possibilities. Including the not-so-far-fetched idea that one of the inventors whose baby I had rejected might be out for vengeance. It wouldn't be the first time! Remind me to tell you sometime about how Pen and I had to dodge a jellylike blob of protoplasm flung at us by an irate professor.

With that experience in mind, I approached the corpse. Slowly. *Very* slowly. The thing is, I don't do real well with dead people. I learned that after stumbling across two decomposing bodies out in the West Texas desert. They were pretty ripe when I found them. This guy wasn't—yet—but you can understand my reluctance to get too close.

Foster rolled him over just enough for us to see his face. His features were still more or less intact. Enough for me to assert with some certainty that I'd never seen him before.

Not so for Sergeant Roth. She sucked in air, big time, and went as white as her bandages.

"Oh, God! I . . . I . . ."

She swayed, her eyes huge with dismay.

"I know him," she got out in a ragged whisper. "We were . . . We were stationed together in Afghanistan."

CHAPTER THREE

ROTH'S startling admission hung in the air for several seconds. Then Officer Foster whipped out his black notebook again while I spun around to take another gander at the dead guy.

He wasn't a pretty sight, but there was enough left to guess he was in his early to mid-thirties and had been pretty buff before a three-and-a-half-ton SUV flattened him.

"His name . . . His name is Austin," Roth said unsteadily. "Oliver Austin."

Foster scribbled furiously in his little black book. "And you say you were in the same unit in Afghanistan?"

"The same base, not the same unit. We . . . We hung out together between shifts sometimes."

"So you were friends?"

"For a while."

"Only awhile?"

"Ollie was . . ."

She stopped. Wet her lips. Turned wide, dismayed eyes on the corpse. A dozen emotions seemed to flit across her face, none of them particularly pleasant.

"Ollie was intense. Too intense for me. I was relieved when he rotated back to the States."

She paused again, obviously struggling with the brutal fact that a former comrade in arms had just taken aim at her. Foster waited a few moments before giving her a nudge.

"Did you stay in touch with Austin after he rotated back to the States?"

"He emailed me a few times. I . . . Uh . . ."

She raised a hand to her cheek again and fingered the bandages. Pulling in a ragged breath, she made a heroic effort to compose herself.

"I didn't reply. Before he left, I told him that I needed to focus on my kids when I got home and get reacquainted with them after being gone so long. I thought he'd taken the hint when the emails stopped."

She looked up then, and her eyes flooded with a guilt so raw it seemed to take over her face.

"After I reported in to Fort Bliss," she said on a note of pure anguish, "I heard Ollie had been diagnosed with PTSD and medically separated from the Army."

Oh, Christ! Post-traumatic stress disorder. I haven't served in a combat zone but even non'ers like me know the grim statistics impacting those who have. One estimate put the PTSD rate among Iraq and Afghanistan veterans at 15 to 20 percent. The suicide rate was way up there, too.

"I made some calls," Roth continued in a broken voice. "I tracked Ollie to a VA hospital in North Carolina, but . . ."

"But?" Foster prompted when she faltered.

"He was gone. He'd checked himself out and disappeared."

"So you haven't had any contact with him at all since his return?"

"No."

"Did you know he was here, in El Paso?"

"No."

"Have you received any suspicious calls or hangups?"

"No."

Her voice steadied a little more with each response. The cop in her had obviously reasserted itself. Foster was jotting down notes when the arrival of several vehicles drew his attention.

"Good, here's the CSI unit. Our homicide unit should be right behind them. If you and the lieutenant will just wait here . . ."

A cell phone jangled inside the Tahoe. Diane took a quick glance at the watch strapped to her wrist and made an urgent request.

"That's probably my daughter. Or the director of her day-care center. Can I retrieve my phone from the car?"

Foster nodded. "Go ahead. I'll coordinate with CSI."

Roth grabbed the phone, checked caller ID, and had it to her ear on the fourth ring. "Hi, Trish. Yes, baby, I know what time it is. I'm, uh, running late."

She listened a moment, her lower lip caught between her teeth.

"No, I can't come right now to take you to Brownies. I'll try to reach Mrs. Hall and ask her to swing by. What? Okay, put her on."

A resigned expression came over the sergeant's face as she waited.

"Hello, Mrs. Gonzales. I know, I know. I'm really racking up the late charges. It's not my job this time, though. There's been an incident. No, I can't pick them up right now. Yes, I read the notice saying you needed to close early tonight. I'm sorry, you'll just have to . . ."

I made a side-to-side hand movement to catch her attention. Brows raised in query, Roth put her caller on hold.

"Hang on a sec, Mrs. Gonzales."

"Someone from my office could pick the kids up," I suggested. "Or maybe you, Mitch."

He blinked at being volunteered for chauffeur duties but gave a shrug. "Sure."

Roth looked him over from head to toe, assessing his trustworthiness. With his wide shoulders and rugged, Marlboro Man features he certainly didn't fit the stereotypical image of a child predator.

Not that I'm an expert on that particular brand of scum. The closest I've come to one is a cousin in Idaho who reportedly got hot and heavy with a very precocious sixteen-year-old. Until her father discovered who she was slipping out to meet at night, that is. Eddie is now minus one testicle and hoping for parole next year.

I *have* become pretty well acquainted with Special Agent Jeff Mitchell over the past six months, however. I was about to assure Diane Roth of his honesty, integrity, and occasionally warped sense of humor when she reached her own conclusions about his character. Raising her gaze from the badge clipped to his waist, she met his steady look.

"Are you sure you don't mind?"

"I don't mind," he replied in his easy West Texas drawl.

"Thanks." She put her phone to her ear again. "Okay, Mrs. Gonzales. Border Patrol Agent Mitchell will be there in a few minutes to pick up Trisha and Joey."

Had to be tough being a single mom *and* a military cop, I thought as Roth flipped her phone shut.

"I really appreciate this," she said with obvious relief. "I'm on the waiting list for the twenty-four-hour day-care center on post. Until I get the kids in there, it's tough finding sitters and day-care staff willing to work around my shifts. Thank God for my neighbor. I don't know what I would have done without her."

I could sympathize with Sergeant Roth. I'd worked some squirrelly shifts myself during my days as a cocktail waitress in 'round-the-clock Vegas. All I had to factor into my disturbed sleep cycle, though, was a horny spouse. I couldn't imagine having to juggle the needs of two children, then dragging my tail in to work at three a.m.

"They're at the Red Robin Learning Center, only a few blocks from here," Roth told Mitch. "Our apartment is close to the center. If you have a pen, I'll write both addresses for you."

She jotted down the information and worked her mouth into a grateful smile. The effort was almost painful to watch.

"I'll be there as soon as they finish with me and I can arrange transportation."

"I'll drive you home," I volunteered.

The arrangements complete, Mitch tipped us a two-fingered salute and made for his dusty pickup. I followed his progress across the parking lot. So did Sergeant Roth. Not many guys look as good from behind as Jeff Mitchell does.

Roth and I leaned our hips against the fender of the patrol car, and her glance drifted from Mitch's behind to my front. The tubular glasses I'd hooked in the V of my ABU shirt drew a puzzled frown.

"Are those some kind of new equipment item?"

"No." I fingered the sleek optics. "They're a component of an experimental, non-line of sight optical sensing system. I was testing it when I spotted Austin."

"You were conducting a test?" Her gaze swept the mall parking lot. "Here?"

Officer Foster had asked the same question, in pretty much the same dubious tone. I knew I'd hear it again and tried to formulate a response that didn't sound *too* defensive.

"My team and I usually test items submitted for our review at a remote site out on the Fort Bliss range, under more controlled conditions. But this particular system has potential for application in an urban setting so I decided to try it in, er, an urban setting."

That sounded lame even to me, but Roth merely nodded. "Thank God you did!"

I hoped my team would express the same fervent approval. Rocky, our test engineer, gets a little snippy when we don't follow precise protocols. The man has what some might call a compulsive-obsessive personality. God forbid someone should misalign his manuals or adjust the air conditioner plus or minus a few degrees outside his comfort zone.

The homicide detectives arrived while I was contemplating how I'd explain all this to Rocky and the rest of the team. After consulting with Officer Foster, the detectives questioned Sergeant Roth and me separately.

The NLOS system drew a frown and required more explanation than I wanted to give. I didn't exactly lie, but I did hint that the El Paso Police Department should keep the precise details out of their report due to patent considerations and, ahem, national security concerns.

The two detectives spent considerably more time with Diane Roth than they had with me. Not surprising, given her relationship to the deceased. I used the interval to collect the sensors I'd positioned. They were safely back in their egg carton and the glasses once more Bubble-Wrapped when the detectives finally released Diane.

She sank into the passenger seat of the Sebring and propped an elbow on the door frame. Raising a trembling hand, she covered her eyes. The rusty bloodstains on her neck and uniform stood out in stark relief to the white bandages covering her cheek.

"You okay?" I asked, pausing with the key a few inches from the ignition switch.

"Yeah. It's just . . ." She dropped her hand and let out a long, shuddering breath. "Ollie Austin here! In El Paso. Who knows how long he's been stalking me. Or my kids."

That brought her jerking upright in her seat.

"Oh, God! My babies."

"They're safe," I rushed to assure her. "Mitch would have called otherwise."

"No, no. It's not that."

"Then what?"

She hitched a strand of pale blond hair behind her ear and shook her head. "I can just imagine how my ex's parents could twist this . . . this attack around and make it my fault. What perfect ammunition for their custody suit."

"Your former in-laws are fighting for custody of your children?"

"They were," she said bitterly. "Fighting hard. And what makes it worse is that I trusted them. I believed their promise to take good care of Trish and Joey while

I was deployed. Not that I had much choice. I didn't have anyone else to leave them with."

"What about their father?"

Her lip curled. "Yeah, right."

"Uh-oh. Sounds like you didn't have any more luck in the husband department than I did."

"You got that right. Alan didn't want our first baby. He gave me a ration every time I had training or worked weekends and he had to play mommy."

Thinking that Diane Roth had faced some tough hurdles, I keyed the ignition and got the Sebring headed out of the parking lot. The Franklins were dark shadows now, barely distinguishable against the deepening purple sky. A suitable backdrop, it turned out, for the grim tale she related.

"Alan and I called it quits when I got pregnant again. His parents blamed me for the split, of course. Or more correctly, they blamed my military career. They thought I should quit the military and take a nine-to-five office job. Like I'm going to turn my back on all my years of training and time in service? Besides that, I'm a good cop. Damned good."

I believed her. Judging by her actions this evening, the woman had nerves of tempered steel.

"Alan took himself out of the daddy picture completely when he fell asleep at the wheel," she related with a shake of her head. "The highway patrol estimated he was whizzing along at eighty-five miles an hour when he sideswiped another car and rolled down an embankment. He died on the way to the hospital."

Ouch! I could relate to that. My grandfather had passed out at the wheel of a semi after downing the better part of a bottle of bourbon.

"The in-laws blamed me for that, too. But they stayed close to their only grandkids." Her mouth twisted. "So close they decided they could provide a more stable home environment than I could. My tour in Afghanistan gave them just the fodder they needed to initiate custody proceedings."

"You're kidding! Surely no court would even *consider* taking away your kids while you were serving in a combat zone."

"You think?" She gave a harsh laugh. "Alan's folks had money. Lots of it. They shelled out megabucks to find a loophole in the amendment Congress passed last year."

"What amendment?"

"A fix to the Servicemembers Civil Relief Act. It's supposed to prevent initiation of child custody proceedings while a military man or woman is deployed. But that didn't stop my in-laws from trying."

Her mouth tight, she scrubbed the heel of her hand against her uninjured temple.

"I spent almost my entire fifteen months in Afghanistan wrangling long distance with lawyers. I had to stand in line for hours waiting for a phone to talk to them. And to talk to my kids. When I finally got through, my bitch of a mother-in-law would tell me they were over at a friend's or out riding their bikes or gone for ice cream with their granddad."

I'd only just met the woman, but I shared her anger. What a rotten thing to pull on someone dodging bullets in a combat zone.

"But it's over now?" I said after a moment.

"Yeah." Her hand dropped. Releasing a long breath, she turned toward the window. "It's over now."

I chewed on what she'd told me while we drove the few short blocks to her apartment. I wasn't a parent. Had never even been pregnant, knock on wood. But the inherent unfairness of using a woman's involuntary deployment to a combat zone as justification for trying to take away her children really pissed me off.

My righteous indignation on behalf of all military women was tempered by the sneaking suspicion that a good number of men in uniform had probably faced the same challenge from ex-spouses or seemingly well-intentioned grandparents. And here I'd spent most of my military career in (relatively) safe El Paso, complaining about outdated air-conditioning systems. Diane's problems sure put mine in perspective.

We pulled into her apartment complex a short time later. It was one of those monster subdivisions, much newer and bigger than mine. The seemingly endless blocks of four- and six-apartment units were done in white, rose, or tan adobe. Fountains and pools and playgrounds invited residents to mingle in open spaces strategically placed among the buildings and rows of covered parking spaces.

Diane had the end unit in a two-story, rose-tinted building. When we went inside, it was immediately apparent the place housed two lively children. Toys and storybooks were scattered everywhere, along with backpacks and sneakers and bright-colored jackets.

Mitch sat on the sofa with a youngster on either side while Disney cartoon characters danced on the TV screen. The older of the two kids, a ponytailed girl of about seven or eight, jumped off the sofa when she saw her mother and ran into her outstretched arms.

"Mommy! Mr. Mitch told us you had an accident. He said you weren't hurt but . . . but . . ."

Tears spurted from her eyes as she took in the bandages and bloodstained uniform.

"I'm okay, Trish. Honest." Diane cradled her daughter against her good side, smoothing a tumble of curls the same pale champagne color as her own. "All I got were a few cuts from broken glass."

Reassured, the girl pulled back with a sniffle. "Mr. Mitch said our car was smashed."

"It was."

The tears pooled again. "How're you gonna take me to dance class tomorrow?"

"We'll work something out. Joey, baby, come give Mommy a kiss."

I got a funny twinge watching the toddler waddle over to his mother. I'm pretty sure my maternal gene is severely constrained, if not totally deficient. Good thing, too, as my family is totally dysfunctional. My alcoholic mother certainly didn't set much of an example and watching my siblings battle with their various offspring over the years had pretty much nixed any desire in me to engage in similar skirmishes. My brief marriage to Charlie Dumbass Spade had only underscored the wisdom of that decision.

Yet seeing the joy in Diane's eyes as her son reached for her with chubby arms stirred all kinds of sensations. Weird sensations. Like a sort of empty feeling. And a little stab of envy.

Not just in me, I realized when I caught the way Mitch's expression went closed and tight. He was thinking of his daughter, I knew.

Mitch rarely talked about the fourteen-year-old who lived with her mother in Seattle. Or the grim circumstances that forced him to stay away from Jenny for her own protection. In the months he and I had been seeing each other, though, I'd come to understand how deep the hurt of that enforced separation went.

"Well," I said after Diane had nuzzled her son's neck and elicited a round of high-pitched giggles, "I guess we'd better go."

She pushed to her feet and held out her hand. "Thank you. Again."

"You're welcome." I returned her strong, sure grip. "Again."

After all we'd been through together, I hated to leave her without wheels. "Do you need a ride to work tomorrow? My team and I are scheduled to depart for our test site at the crack of dawn but I could swing by early and drive you to the post."

"I should be okay. My car insurance covers a rental. I'll call Enterprise tonight and set something up. But I appreciate the offer." She turned to Mitch. "And I appreciate you taking care of these two imps."

"My pleasure." A slow smile crinkled the skin at the corners of his eyes. "First time I've seen *The Princess and the Frog*. I'll have to guess how it ends."

Ponytailed Trish piped up with a gracious offer. "You kin take the DVD 'n' watch it, if you want. Joey 'n' me already know how it ends."

"That's okay. I'll catch it some other time around. 'Night, guys."

"'Night."

Mitch and I were quiet as we walked out of Diane's apartment into the starry February night. The temperature had dropped with the sun and a brisk wind swept in off the high desert.

"Mind if we skip Perry's?" I asked as we approached our separate vehicles. "I'm not in the mood for noise. How about we order a large pepperoni to go and chow down at my place instead?"

He skimmed a glance over my face. I must have looked like I'd just helped take down a would-be assassin or something, because he backed out of pizza altogether.

"You need to decompress. Better you go home and get some sleep."

I suspected the tight expression I'd glimpsed inside the house a few moments ago might have something to do with his calling it a night. As I said, he doesn't talk about his past much. But I know he'd turned to booze after he'd been forced to cut off all ties with his ex-wife and daughter to keep them safe from the vicious killer who'd sworn revenge against Mitch by going after his family.

He was off the booze now. Had been since well before we met. The hurt was still there, though.

"How long will you be out at the site?" he asked.

"We're scheduled for ten days."

"You coming home over the weekend?"

"I don't think so. Our agenda's pretty crammed. This is the first time we've gone fully operational since the fire at the lab."

"Then I'll see you when I see you."

I reminded myself this was exactly what we both wanted from our still evolving relationship. Stimulating companionship. Mutual understanding of the demands of our respective careers. Really hot sex every time the opportunity presented itself, which evidently wasn't the case tonight.

Nodding, I lifted my mouth to his. "I'll see you when I see you."

CHAPTER FOUR

MUCH as I hated to miss out on an evening with my sexy Border Patrol agent, I have to admit my tail was dragging when I pulled up at my apartment. Getting caught in a lethal cross fire sure takes it out of you.

Retrieving the NLOS system from the Sebring's trunk, I lugged it from the parking space to my front door. I rent a one bedroom, one bath in a military-friendly complex located twenty minutes from Fort Bliss's west gate. Most of the residents are singles like me or young couples from the post. The gregarious crowd makes for lively Friday and Saturday evenings out by the pool. So lively, bathing suits have been known to become optional on occasion.

My comfy if somewhat messy apartment always gives me a feeling of intense satisfaction. Took me a while to figure out why. I now know it's a delayed response to those twelve weeks of hell otherwise known as officers' training school. Talk about life-altering experiences!

If asked, I would've categorized myself as a relatively neat person before I shipped out to OTS. All those weeks of cupping my bras and folding my panties into precise, three-inch squares shattered that illusion forever.

So can you blame me if I dropped the NLOS carton on the coffee table? And tossed my hat on the next nearest horizontal surface? And hitched my ABU blouse on the back of a chair? Each of us has to assert our individuality in our own ways.

Sorting through my mail took all of three minutes. The bills I tossed aside. The stack of glam mags I carried with me into the bedroom. My boots came off next and were left to lie where they hit. My pants landed in a heap. They were followed by my standard-issue yucky brown T-shirt and sports bra. I suffered a pang of real regret as I shed the sleek hipsters I'd worn in anticipation of a post-pizza session with Mitch, but the tight knot of tension at the base of my skull indicated he'd been right on target. I needed to decompress.

I was up to my chin in scented bubbles and perusing the latest issue of *Allure* when the cell phone I'd positioned within reach jangled. I checked the caller ID, saw it was Pen, and flipped up the lid. Her face filled the screen, topped by wide eyes and her loose, lopsided bun. She usually fastens the topknot with pens, pencils, chopsticks, whatever's handy. The implement sticking out of her salt-and-pepper hair tonight defied definition.

"I just saw the nine o'clock news on Fox!"

"Never mind the news. What's in your hair?"

She patted around her bun and extracted a meat thermometer. The kind with a long, pointed stem and a round face for reading degrees of doneness.

"So that's where it went to," she said on a surprised note. "I cooked a tofu and chickpea loaf for supper and looked all over for this thing."

"Pen!" Gulping, I watched her stab it into the bun again. "Be careful with that."

"Yes, yes. But let's get back to the news. I just heard a report that two women from Fort Bliss were involved in a shooting incident. When the newscaster mentioned that one of the women was an Air Force lieutenant, I was worried it might be you."

"It was."

"I knew it! You're all right, aren't you?"

"I'm fine."

"The report gave only sketchy details. What happened?"

"The police are still sorting through evidence. Right now, though, it looks like a vet suffering from PTSD came after the female soldier who rejected him. I, uh, just happened to be in the vicinity."

"Ha!"

Pen has this unique laugh. It's a cross between a

51

snuffling snort and a high-pitched whinny. When you add sarcasm to the mix, the sound makes even the most stalwart among us wince.

"Things never 'just happen' around you, Samantha."

I squirmed in my bubbles for a moment. "Okay, I might have been trying out the NLOS system that came in this afternoon and sort of spotted the shooter."

Not surprisingly, she zeroed in on my reluctant admission. "You conducted a test? Without observers or the proper protocols?"

Another squishy squirm. "It wasn't an official test."

"Obviously. Rocky's *not* going to be happy about this."

Rocky wasn't. He beeped in while I was still on the line with Pen. I hung up on her and took his call. With great reluctance, I might add. After assuring my erstwhile test engineer that I was, in fact, the female Air Force lieutenant named on the news, I mentioned the NLOS tryout. I figured I might as well, since Pen would blab to the rest of the team anyway.

I finally calmed Rocky down and disconnected, only to have the phone chirp again in my hand. Sighing, I went through the same litany with Dennis O'Reilly, then Sergeant Cassidy. Every last bubble had disintegrated by the time I finally climbed out of the tub and caught the tail end of the ten p.m. news.

The police hadn't released the identity of the deceased yet, but an enterprising news crew had ferreted out Diane Roth's name and military background. A picture of her in uniform flashed up on the TV screen. Serious and unsmiling, she still managed to look feminine and attractive. No small feat, as any woman who clumps around in combat boots day after day will attest.

"According to witnesses," the newscaster intoned, "Sergeant Roth risked her own life to save theirs."

The camera cut to a heavyset male in a blue jogging suit. The same one I'd last seen kissing the pavement outside the fitness center.

"She's a hero," he asserted, blinking owlishly in the glare of klieg lights. "An honest-to-God hero. The rest of us scrambled for cover, scared out of our gourds. Sergeant Roth was the only one who took action. No telling how many people might have been killed or wounded if she hadn't."

THE story dominated the early morning news, as well. Coffee cup in hand, I watched as a startled Diane Roth opened her front door the next morning and was confronted by a phalanx of media.

She handled herself well. That cop training again, no doubt. After her first, surprised reaction, she shooed her kids back into her apartment and calmly refused to answer the questions hurled at her by reporters.

"I'm sorry, I'm an MP. I'm also part of the ongoing investigation. I'm sure you understand that I can't comment on it."

I gave a distinctly Pen-like snort. No way that would stem the barrage. I've had a taste of how these guys operate. Sure enough the questions kept coming.

"Is it true you knew the shooter?"

"Were you his target?"

"What was his name?"

"Please. I'm not cleared to give any statement to the press."

"Cleared?"

"Before I speak to the media, I need to check with my supervisor and the public affairs office on post."

And the JAG, I added mentally. As a potential victim and the perpetrator of a violent death, she'd have to be very careful what she said to whom.

I knew the Army's Criminal Investigation Division would conduct its own investigation into last night's incident. Having come into contact with a certain CID agent in the Fort Bliss detachment when my lab got torched, I felt nothing but sympathy for Diane Roth. Which was why I winced when she dropped my name.

"All the witnesses we've interviewed say you're a hero, Sergeant Roth. That you saved their lives."

"Again, no comment. But I wasn't the only one who took action. Lieutenant Spade risked drawing the gunman's fire when she shouted the warning that saved *my* life."

"What was that name?"

"Spade. Samantha Spade."

Groaning, I dumped my coffee dregs in the sink. It's not that I have anything against TV reporters. They're just doing their job when they rip the flesh off the bones of the poor schmucks they pin in front of a camera.

Profoundly relieved I'd be out of town for the next ten days, I loaded my gear into the Sebring. The early morning temperature hovered around fifty-five. Way too cool to put the top down. I grabbed my ABU jacket from the hall closet and was closing up the apartment when my home phone started ringing.

I let it ring and hit the road.

MY team and I convoyed out to our test site. Dennis and Rocky drove the van loaded with equipment and projects we'd scheduled for testing. Sergeant Cassidy hauled our supplies in his pickup. That left Pen and me free to tool along in my Sebring.

It's just a little over eighty miles out to the site as the crow flies. Those of us without wings have to follow a series of narrow county roads east, then south, then east again. I managed to avoid collecting another speeding ticket. Not for lack of trying, but the gods were on my side this time.

The meandering route leads us to a remote corner of the Fort Bliss test range. It also takes us right through the town of Dry Springs, Texas. Dry Springs is just that. Completely, totally parched. Spring, summer, fall, and winter. I'm told it may get a quarter inch or so of rain once or twice a year. If so, I sure haven't seen it!

The town itself consists of a cluster of crumbling adobe buildings. One of them is a combination motel, convenience store, cafe, and bar called Pancho's. The place has become a compulsory stop for FST-3 both going out to and returning from our test site.

Pen and I arrived first. Naturally. That Sebring is sweeeeet! When we pulled into the dirt parking lot and trooped into the cafe/bar side of Pancho's, a barrage of familiar scents assaulted us. I ignored the lingering cigarette smoke and stale, musty smell of the crushed pistachio shells on the floor. Instead, my nose zeroed in on the spicy bouquet emanating from the pot of green chili stew Pancho keeps bubbling seven days a week.

The proprietor himself was swiping down the wooden counter that ran the length of the place. He peered at us with his right eye—a black patch obscures the left—and twitched his bushy black mustache into a wide grin.

"*Hola*, Lieutenant!"

"*Hola*, Pancho."

"Good to see you. And you, Penelope."

I've heard several different versions of how Pancho lost his eye. Some say it was in a riot after a soccer match in Mexico. Others contend that one of his wives ground a thumb in the socket in a fit of jealousy. Since he's not talking and he left any and all wives behind when he hightailed it out of Mexico, no one can verify either version.

I tend to lean toward the second theory, however. Mostly because Pancho has a thing for the ladies. You can deduce this from his bar's decor. Decades worth of *Sports Illustrated* Swimsuit Edition covers obliterate almost every square inch of the walls and ceiling.

Oddly enough, the ladies have a thing for Pancho, too. Maybe it's the twinkle in his good eye. Or the flash of white teeth under his handlebar mustache. Whatever it is, every female under the age of ninety who enters his establishment is expected to give him a ritual kiss on the cheek. Even Pen, who's not normally prone to public displays of affection.

After the requisite buss, Pancho poured coffee for me and rooted around under the counter for the tea canister he keeps for Pen. She imbibes the most gawdawful stuff and is always pestering the rest of the team to do the same. We try to hold out, but after a few days at the site she usually wears down our resistance with frequent lectures on the benefits of herbal infusions.

"Heard your name tossed around on the news this morning," Pancho commented as he nudged the tin toward Pen. "Sounds like you had a little excitement last night."

"Just a little."

"What's the story?"

I told him what I knew but cautioned him against sharing it with his other customers. I didn't want to get crosswise of any investigation the Fort Bliss CID guys might be conducting. Again.

Thoughtfully, Pancho stroked his mustache. "Lot of that PTSD going around these days. A trucker passed through a few weeks ago. Told me he had a son who couldn't take the nightmares. Kid slashed his wrists and bled out in a car parked in his old man's driveway."

"Oh, man. What a thing to do to your parent."

I don't remember my father and have this love–barely tolerate–love relationship with my mother. I might leave a voodoo doll with pins stuck in it on her doorstep after one of those marathon sessions when she catalogues all my faults, but I wouldn't bleed out in her driveway. Not by choice, anyway.

The rest of the team arrived a few minutes later. After the general bustle of greetings and dishing out bowls of stew, Pancho took Pen into the convenience store side of the place to write down her order for organic produce while I tried to put the grim topic of PTSD out of my head.

IT returned with a vengeance later that afternoon.

My team and I were still in the process of unpacking and setting up operations in Chuville. That's one of our more polite designations for the cluster of Containerized Housing Units that constitute our test site.

The military uses CHUs for offices and troop housing at forward bases. They're aluminum boxes, about eight feet wide by twenty feet long, which doesn't make for a whole lot of living *or* working space. But they're insulated and air-conditioned, and they come with a door, a window, an air vent, and power cabling.

We have five CHUs at our test site. The three men on the team sleep in one. Pen and I share another. (In case you're wondering, Dr. England snorts and whinnies while awake *and* asleep.)

A third CHU serves as our combination rec center and D-FAC. That's military jargon for dining facility, which used to be called a chow hall. Before that it was the mess hall. You can guess why they changed the terminology. Our D-FAC/rec area contains a small kitchen, a miniscule eating area, a TV with a satellite dish, and a Universal Gym. The gym is Staff Sergeant Cassidy's exclusive domain. The rest of us prefer more sedentary pursuits.

The remaining two CHUs are linked together to form our administrative center and test lab. They arrived on site a few months ago to replace our torched units. We had to replace much of our equipment and computers, too.

Hate to admit it, but the arsonist actually did us a favor. My boss came through with some of the newest and latest in test equipment. Rocky begged, badgered, and cajoled the rest from his former associates at headquarters. Our reconstituted lab now contains enough computers and super-high-tech equipment to measure the speed and intensity of a supernova, or so Rocky assures me.

Sergeant Cassidy and I had unlocked the storage shed behind the lab and were gassing up the two ATVs stored there when my cell phone launched into "The Eyes of Texas." I dug it out of my pocket, glanced at the screen display, and grimaced.

"What?" Noel asked.

I aimed the display in his direction. "Detachment Six, CID."

"Don't answer it!"

Sergeant Cassidy had previous personal contact with criminal investigators. They weren't what you would term friendly encounters.

I should mention here that Noel is six feet, three inches of really beefed-up muscle. With two combat tours under his belt, he was on his way up the ranks in the exclusive Special Ops community until he propositioned a sweet young thing.

Turns out *she* was a not-so-young *he* working undercover with the John Squad. Noel beat the solicitation rap but is still trying to recover from the blow of discovering he got all hot and bothered for a guy in net stockings and spike heels. Hence his aversion to criminal investigators of any size, shape, or variety.

Based on my one previous contact with the breed, I wasn't all that much fonder of them. I debated letting the call switch to voice mail. Common sense won out. I'd have to talk to them sooner or later.

"Lieutenant Spade."

"This is Special Agent Andrew Hurst."

Eyes closed, I summoned a mental image of Andy Hurst. He was so rail thin and intense I'd dubbed him Scrawny Guy at our first meeting. The eight or nine strands of straw-colored hair he scraped across his otherwise bald pate had quickly changed his nom de plume to Comb-Over Guy.

"I need to speak to you, Lieutenant. Can you come to my office?"

"Sorry. My team and I are at our test site."

"For how long?"

"We just arrived and are setting up now."

"For how long?" he bit out.

"Ten days," I bit back. Can you tell I don't like this guy?

"I'll drive out there. Give me three hours."

The connection went dead.

"Great," I muttered to Noel. "Special Agent Hurst is gonna pay us a visit."

"Us?" he echoed, throwing me a narrow glance from his hunkered-down position beside one of the ATVs.

"Okay, me."

"He wants to talk to you about the shooting last night?"

"He didn't say, but that's my guess."

Noel mumbled something unintelligible under his breath. I didn't ask for a translation.

You would think the gods would be kind to someone who'd recently dodged bullets. Who rushed to the aid of a sister in arms. Someone who'd just relocated to the backside of beyond.

Not so. "The Eyes of Texas" belted out again just a few moments later.

"Oh, no," I groaned. "It's Dr. J."

"Don't answer it!" Noel said again.

This time I followed his advice. I like my boss. I really do. What's more, I respect him tremendously. I mean, how many people do you know who've earned a string of degrees a mile long? And served two terms as president of the National Institutes of Health's Black

Scientists Association, besides being a fellow at Harvard's prestigious Center for the Study of Science, Technology, and Public Policy?

The problem is, Dr. David Jessup accepted a position as a program manager in DARPA's Tactical Technology Division the same week my boss at the Air Force Weapons Laboratory shuffled me off to DARPA. Dr. J still isn't quite sure how he got stuck supervising me, a lowly lieutenant at the end of a very long leash. Neither am I. Suffice to say, we tread warily when dealing with each other. Which is why I listened carefully when his call went to voice mail.

"Samantha, this is David Jessup. An agent from the Office of Special Investigations just stopped by my office."

Uh-oh. The OSI is the Air Force's counterpart to the Army's CID. This wasn't good. The last time the OSI had visited Dr. J was after my lab got torched. He and I had both ended up churning out reams of reports. *Not* an experience I wanted to repeat anytime soon.

"The agent informed me that you were involved in a shooting incident in El Paso last night. He also informed me you weren't hurt. I'm not sure why I had to hear this from him and not you," Dr. J continued in a pained voice, "but I'm relieved you escaped injury. Please call me and tell me what the hell is going on."

Double uh-oh! That was a first. Dr. J never resorted to expletives. Acting as my supervisor must be exerting more pressure on the man than I'd realized.

When he disconnected, I was left with the uneasy

feeling that forces beyond my control had me in a slowly tightening vise. I didn't appreciate *how* tight until Special Agent Hurst drove up to the site three hours later in a dust-covered sedan.

CHAPTER FIVE

HURST brought some backup with him. Both investigators wore civilian clothes. I guessed their khaki Dockers and open-necked shirts topped by casual sport coats were supposed to project a friendly, approachable air. It didn't fool me for a moment.

I met them outside the lab. The February afternoon had warmed up. So much so that I spotted an orange-and-silver snake basking in the sunlight a few yards from our lab. I knew it was a nonpoisonous Mexican king snake. Pen had lectured us often enough on the flora and fauna of the Chihuahuan Desert. Still, I cut it a wide swath when I went to greet the two investigators.

Comb Over did the intros. "Lieutenant Spade, this is Special Agent Richard Sinclair from CID headquarters. They're handling the Austin investigation."

I wondered why the case had been bumped up to the guys at headquarters as Sinclair showed me his credentials. He was a few inches shorter than my five-seven and built like a tank. He also had laser blue eyes and a bruiser grip.

"Where can we talk?" Comb Over asked.

"The rest of my team is powering up and calibrating equipment in the lab. We can use the D-FAC."

My team had put away the perishables, but cartons of unloaded supplies still crowded the counters. The cartons gave me an uneasy, hemmed-in feeling as I faced the investigators across the small dining table.

Sinclair placed a palm-sized tape recorder on the table. "We'd like to record this session, unless you object."

"Should I?"

Some nasty thoughts buzzed around inside my head. Chief among them was the fact that I'd conducted an unauthorized test. In a civilian setting. Under uncontrolled conditions. I was fully prepared to argue the test hadn't resulted in any toxic fallout and had, in fact, possibly saved several lives when Sinclair reassured me.

"You're not the subject of this investigation, if that's what you're asking."

His comment eased my nagging conscience. A little.

"Please tell us in your own words, Lieutenant, exactly what happened."

I didn't bother to point out that I'd already given statements to the first officers on the scene and the homicide detectives who'd caught the case. As Mitch had laconically explained, cops liked to give witnesses and/or suspects plenty of opportunity to trip over their own words.

I managed not to trip. I think. I also managed to downplay the whole NLOS thing. Sinclair didn't seem particularly interested in *how* I spotted Austin. His focus was on what happened once I had.

"Let me be sure I understand the sequence," he said when I'd finished. "You say a bullet shattered Sergeant Roth's car window?"

"Correct."

"At which point you shouted another warning?"

"Also correct."

"And that's when she spotted Austin?"

"Right."

"Then she accelerated and aimed her vehicle in his direction?"

"Her Tahoe rolled toward the fitness center at first," I said, my forehead scrunching as I tried to recall those terrifying seconds. "Diane—Sergeant Roth—had dropped down, out of my sight. I thought she'd been hit. I remember jumping up and sprinting toward her vehicle. I was afraid it would cream the people who'd flattened themselves against the pavement."

"You ran toward the Tahoe? That wasn't in the report you gave the El Paso PD last night."

"I was still a little frazzled when I gave my statement. I guess I forgot that minor detail. It doesn't matter anyway, since Diane yanked on the wheel and aimed it at the white van shielding the shooter."

Sinclair tapped a finger against the tabletop for a moment or two, a carefully neutral expression in those electric blue eyes.

"You stated that when Sergeant Roth crashed into the van, the rear end of her Tahoe fishtailed and slammed Austin against the wall."

"Right."

"And after he crumpled, she backed her vehicle over him."

"Right. But she couldn't have seen him. He fell directly behind that monster SUV. And ... And everything happened so fast."

Not the best defense against vehicular manslaughter or excessive use of force, I know, but you had to be there.

"To tell the truth, Agent Sinclair, I'm still amazed that Diane pulled it together and reacted as fast as she did. If Austin was after her, it's a clear case of self-defense. She saved not only her own life but any number of innocent bystanders."

"Judging by the headlines Agent Hurst showed me this morning," Sinclair said dryly, "that seems to be the public consensus."

"So tell me," I countered. "*Was* Austin after her?"

I didn't hold much hope of getting a straight answer out of him. Sure enough, he dodged the question.

"Sorry. I can't reveal the details of an ongoing investigation."

"Then tell me this. Why is CID HQ running this

show? Why not Comb . . ." I caught myself just in time. Heroically, I managed to refrain from glancing at the sparse strands plastered across Andrew Hurst's shiny dome while I covered my near-slip. "Why not the commander of our local CID detachment?"

Blue Eyes drummed his finger on the table again before doling out a reluctant nugget of information.

"Oliver Austin was the subject of another investigation regarding certain events that occurred while he was in Afghanistan. It's my job to tie up the loose ends."

Interesting. Diane had mentioned that Austin was intense. So intense she'd decided to ease out of any association with the man once she rotated back to the States. I figured she'd already made that point to the investigators, however, and kept my mouth shut.

"One last question, Lieutenant. Did Sergeant Roth give any indication that she knew the identity of the shooter before she took him out?"

"Absolutely not. He was wearing a ski mask and, as I said, partially obscured by the van. Neither she nor I got a look at him until one of the responding officers rolled his body over. When Diane saw his face, she went dead white. I thought she was going to keel over in shock."

Blue Eyes considered that in silence for a moment before clicking off the recorder.

"All right. Thanks for your cooperation. Here's my card. If you remember any other details you think might be pertinent to the investigation, give me or Special Agent Hurst a call."

Nodding, I pocketed the card. "Will do."

AFTER seeing the two agents off, I broke down and returned my boss's call. Given the two-hour time difference, I figured Dr. J would have left for the day. Thankfully, I figured right. With any luck I'd have some positive—and very official—test results to distract him with by the time we connected tomorrow.

WITH that goal in mind, I dragged out of the CHU I shared with Pen just after seven thirty the following morning. It always takes me several nights to acclimate to her nocturnal snuffles and snorts. Consequently I wasn't feeling my usual chipper self when I entered the D-FAC in search of breakfast.

"'Morning, Geardo Goddess."

That came from O'Reilly, of course. I grunted in return.

"Pen up?"

"She's right behind me."

The guys hastily gulped down their respective cups of coffee. My lips pooched when I saw they hadn't left enough in the pot for me.

"Thanks," I muttered, shooting them evil glares as Pen entered and promptly emptied the dregs to brew hot water for the infusion she'd steeped overnight. We all trooped over to the lab a half hour later with our taste buds shrieking from her special combination of chrysanthemum and the inner bark of the pau d'arco tree.

At my insistence, we'd put the NLOS system at the top of the agenda. I was determined to get it right this time and—oh, by the way—defuse any potential fallout from the unauthorized test.

Once the components were unpacked, Dennis duly recorded their specifications in our computerized test log. Meanwhile Rocky and Pen worked some kind of technical magic that would allow our instrumentation to capture and analyze the interactive signals. That left Sergeant Cassidy and me to scatter the sensors and conduct the test.

I kept a wary eye out for the king snake I'd spotted yesterday as I crunched over the hard-packed dirt to deposit the shiny disks behind the saguaro and stubby mesquite surrounding our site. Noel took his disks farther afield.

I don't know if you've driven through or maybe spent a weekend camping in the Chihuahuan Desert. It stretches across more than two hundred thousand square miles from West Texas and Arizona to as far south as Mexico City. Those miles encompass dozens of different topographies, from blinding white gypsum flats to towering peaks.

Our site sits perched atop a dusty plateau cut by deep arroyos and punctuated by granite outcroppings the locals call "sky islands." The upthrust granite, my team had collectively decided, would serve as obstacles for the NLOS system to see around, over, or through. Since I'd pretty much compromised my objectivity last night, I designated Noel to act as the test subject.

"Ready?" I asked when we'd scattered the sensors and he'd located the switch on the glasses.

"Ready."

"Okay," I radioed the others. "We're good to go."

"Fire 'em up," Dennis instructed.

Noel flicked the switch to remotely activate the sensors.

"We're receiving a signal," Dennis relayed. "Make that several signals. What have you got at your end?"

"Nothing yet. Noel's just putting on the goggles now."

His massive shoulders hunching, Sergeant Cassidy squinted through the narrow slit.

"I don't see anything except mesquite."

"Wait."

I had begun to worry that I'd somehow damaged the system when he suddenly yelped and threw up his hands as if to ward off an attack.

"Holy Christ!"

Staggering, he lunged backward.

"Noel, watch out!"

My warning came too late. He tripped over a clump of spiny creosote and went down. I was treated to some colorful and decidedly scatological Special Ops terminology as he whipped off the goggles and tossed them aside. Still swearing, he let me help him up. The tough fabric of our ABUs had protected him from the worst of the stickers. The rest I plucked out.

I have to admit removing stickers from an NCO's behind was a new leadership experience for me. I'd never envisioned quite this set of circumstances when my instructors at officers' training school had droned on and on about taking care of your troops.

It must have been a new experience for Noel, too, because he turned brick red and didn't meet my eyes when he muttered a gruff, "Thanks."

I let him recover while I retrieved the goggles. "Want to give it another go?"

He eyed the slender tube with a distinct lack of enthusiasm. "I guess so."

"Select one image to focus on, then turn your head to follow that image."

Easier said than done, he discovered in the frustrating forty-five minutes that followed. Noel gave it his best shot but gave up when he got so dizzy I thought he was going to pass out.

I took a turn with the goggles next. The first assault sent me backward, too. As it had the night before, a blinding kaleidoscope of images flooded my line of sight. So bright, the searing colors hurt my eyes. So intense, I instinctively ducked when a twisted branch covered with silvery green leaves seemed to fly right at me.

Despite my best efforts, I couldn't seem to filter the images. I gave it up after a nauseating fifteen minutes and retreated with Noel to the lab.

The five of us stood around the table where I laid the

goggles and retrieved sensors. Rocky brought over printouts of the data he'd recorded.

"I don't understand it," I muttered. "The system worked last night."

"Could be due to different light spectrums," Rocky theorized, pointing to sharp spikes in the data. "And different density of objects to see around or through. Granite would deflect signals with more intensity than a porous brick or concrete."

I had to take his word for that. I chewed on my lower lip, reluctant to relinquish my hope that this system might contribute to Dr. J's much cherished Urban Leader Tactical Response, Awareness, and Visualization Initiative. The basic technology was there. It had worked before. Sort of. We just had to figure out a way to compensate for variables and make it work in all different environments.

Okay, okay. I admit it. I still hoped to get on Dr. J's good side.

"Can we measure the light, factor in the density of obstacles, and try this again?" I asked.

Rocky looked at Pen, who looked at Dennis, who looked back at Rock.

"We've got a spectrometer," my test engineer acknowledged. "But for the kind of precision measurement you're talking about we should really use an interferometer to check the properties of the light waves. And an autocollimator to measure angular deflections."

He worked his mouth from side to side. I hoped that was a signal he was thinking hard and not just twitching his whiskers like a worried hamster. With Dr. Brian Balboa, it's kind of hard to tell.

"I'm not making any promises," he said finally, "but I'll see what I can do."

"Great! We'll try again whenever you're ready. Or whenever the light's right."

We documented the disappointing results and set the NLOS system aside to prep for the next item on our test agenda.

This was a handheld scanner that purported to harness C-band satellite imagery to locate near subsoil moisture in arid locations. The digging tool built into the scanner's handle could then be used to extract potentially life-saving moisture. I reserved judgment until I'd seen the results. I would also refrain from sampling any such extractions until Pen had done a complete chemical analysis.

I learned that lesson the hard way after rubbing on some cream that was *supposed* to blunt the effects of ultraviolet rays. Took weeks for the resulting rash to disappear. Nowadays I don't taste, sniff, or rub on anything until Pen gives it her bioecological stamp of approval.

MY cell phone jangled while we were reviewing the extractor's specifications and finalizing our test parameters. I slipped my cell phone out of my pocket but didn't recognize the number on the display.

I clicked "talk" and brought Diane Roth's image up

on the screen. Bandages still covered the left side of her face. She'd minimized their effect by combing her hair forward, giving her a peekaboo look.

"Hi, Lieutenant. This is Diane Roth."

"Hi, Diane. How are the cuts?"

"Healing. None of them went deep enough to do any real damage."

"That's good to hear."

"Listen, I was a little shook up last night."

"Hmmm. I wonder why."

"Yeah, it was pretty grim. But I don't think I thanked you properly for staying with me and giving me a ride home."

"Sure you did. Several times."

"Still, I'd like to show my appreciation. To you and Agent Mitchell both. I thought maybe the kids and I could treat you to a cookout."

"That's not necessary."

"We'd like to. Really. I owe you, Lieutenant. And the kids enjoyed 'Mr.' Mitch." A wistful note seeped into her voice. "Joey doesn't get to interact all that often with positive male role models. And I think Trish has a world-class crush on the man."

"I'm not surprised. He's eminently crushable."

She cocked her head and looked at me from under the sweep of her hair. "Are you two serious?"

I hesitated. My relationship with Mitch didn't fit into any of my previously defined categories. But then none of the jerks I'd dated—including the one I'd subsequently married—fit into Mitch's category, either.

"I'm sorry," Diane said when my hesitation strung out. "I didn't mean to get personal. Listen, you mentioned last night that you were deploying out to a test site? When do you get back into town?"

"End of next week."

"The kids and I really would like to have you and Mitch over. How about the Saturday afternoon after you get home?"

"I guess that would work. If Mitch is available."

"I'll check with him and call you back to confirm. Oh, and, Lieutenant . . ."

"Yes?"

"You might be contacted by an agent from CID headquarters. He's investigating the incident last night."

"I've already talked to him."

"You have?"

"He drove out to the site this afternoon with an agent from our local detachment."

Another short silence descended. Diane broke it with a wry observation.

"They're sure not wasting any time."

"No, they're not."

"Just as well. My commander has pulled my certification to carry a weapon and put me on administrative duties until the investigation wraps."

"Is that standard procedure?"

"It is." I could almost hear the shrug in her voice. "The kids are happy, anyway. I'm on straight day shifts until this mess is cleared up."

I had a feeling it might take longer to put this incident to bed than either of us had anticipated. Did she know Oliver Austin had been under investigation? Had the guys from CID talked to her about Austin's "questionable activities" in Afghanistan? I started to ask but swallowed the question at the last minute.

I'm not sure what held me back. Nor could I know my silence had just put my life on the line when I nodded and agreed to a Saturday afternoon cookout.

CHAPTER SIX

THE remainder of our sojourn out at the test site was relatively uneventful.

I survived a stiffly polite phone conversation with my boss. Dr. J let me know—in person this time!—that he preferred not to hear from a third party that I'd been shot at. I assured him I hadn't been hurt and promised to apprise him personally of any similar events in the future. I swear I heard him shudder. To my relief, he didn't mention the NLOS system. I certainly didn't bring it up.

I talked to Mitch a couple of times. He mentioned that Diane had contacted him about the cookout. He also mentioned that he'd checked with a buddy at the El Paso PD about the status of the investigation.

"You have?"

"Damn straight. You get shot at, I want to know why."

"Awwwww."

That gave me a warm glow. Perverse, but warm.

"So what does it look like from your perspective?" I asked him.

"Pretty much what it looked like at the scene. PTSD claimed another victim in Austin, almost claimed more in you and Roth and the others."

Mitch had pulled a tour in the Navy before joining the Border Patrol. Enough combat-related stress in both of those fields to explain the gruff edge to his voice.

"What about this cookout?" I asked him. "Are you up for it?"

"If you are. I'm scheduled to work that Saturday, but I can switch shifts. I'll swing by and pick you up."

"It's a date."

BETWEEN all these calls, I worked my buns off. Metaphorically speaking, unfortunately. The team cleared much of the backlog that had built up while our lab was out of operation. Most of the items that had been submitted for our evaluation either (a) didn't perform as promised, (b) didn't perform at all, or (c) were slick as spit and fun to play with but didn't have even the remotest possible applicability to military operations.

We tagged several items for further evaluation. One was the NLOS system. Another was an instrument the inventor had labeled an Olfactory Somatosensory Indicator.

The thing looked like one of those handheld credit card swipers a lot of restaurants and rental car companies use these days. The kind that spits out a paper receipt on the spot. Only this one had a long, thin wand attached and instead of calculating credit card charges, it measured body odors.

I know, I know! I almost choked on my herbal tea when I'd first read the specs. But we've tested weirder inventions. The biologist who'd devised the olfactory sensometer—which we instantly rechristened the Sniffometer—claimed it would measure and categorize scents emanating from any living, secreting primate. Something to do with the proteins encoded in said primate's major histocompatibility complex.

Pen tried to explain MHC but left me in the dust after, oh, thirty or forty seconds. All I got out of her lecture was that most living creatures emit unique odors. So unique that penguins can identify their chicks amid the thousands nesting in huge rookeries and bloodhounds can track an escaping convict for hundreds of miles.

Pen also stressed that these odors are situational. Fear, joy, untruthfulness, sexual arousal, physical exertion—any number of factors could alter our emissions. I certainly didn't need a double PhD to tell me that. I emit situational odors in those instances, too.

Despite her explanation, I harbored distinct doubts about the Sniffometer. Yet I could see its potential for military application. *If* it could in fact differentiate and categorize body odors, it might aid in the interrogation of prisoners. Or identify workplace stress factors. Or allow a squad leader to assess a subordinate's emotional state before, during, or after a mission.

Perhaps even predict an incidence of post-traumatic stress disorder among troops.

With Oliver Austin and the shooting incident still vivid in my mind, I had my team conduct a battery of tests. Pen, Noel, Dennis, and I all took turns as subjects. Rocky demurred, insisting he needed to remain impartial to record and analyze the results. I suspected he was worried he might get too nervous about having his body odors measured and cut loose with one of his world-class bloopers.

Pen went first. We wanded her at work, while she was attempting to make sense of the results of another test; at noon, while she was downing her organic kale, mushroom, and tomato salad; and at dusk, when she returned from her daily commune with nature. We even toted the Sniffometer into our CHU at night and wanded her in her sleep.

I shouldn't have been surprised that her little paper printout showed she emitted almost identical odor types and levels no matter what activity she engaged in. We should all be as emotionally stable as Dr. Penelope England.

Dennis O'Reilly went next. We tried the same variations—at work, at rest, during recreation. Talk about wildly skewed results!

Have I mentioned that Dennis is into chess? Reeeally into chess. Some might term him an aficionado. When he's online, duking it out with another player a half a world away, the term I prefer is royal pain in the ass. The man moans. He swears. He thrusts his hands through his frizzy hair and glowers at the screen until he finally decides on his move. When he captures an opponent's piece, he cackles like a mongoose on steroids. (Pen's description, not mine. I've never encountered a mongoose, on or off steroids.)

Needless to say, Dennis's odors during an online tournament were all over the place and so wildly contradictory Rocky declared his test results inconclusive.

Ditto with me. In my case, I think the Hawthorne effect came into play. I'd first heard about the effect in one of my night courses at UNLV. Seems that when a subject knows he's being watched or measured, he'll invariably alter his behavior despite every urging to act naturally. That really messed up attempts to measure productivity until someone figured out what was happening.

I can't imagine why I remembered that bit of management lore. God knows I forgot everything else in Advanced Business Concepts. But there I was, trying so hard to act nonchalant and ignore the fact that my team was recording my bodily odors that my very determination to remain detached invalidated the results.

Sergeant Cassidy was the only one it seemed to work on. At first. Noel registered a normal range of emissions during the day and went off the charts during his nightly workout. No Hawthorne effect there. The guy is a glutton for sweat. Shiny drops glistened on his bulging muscles and ran in rivulets down his chest as he clanked the weights in a hypnotic rhythm. He'd gotten so into his zone that he didn't so much as notice us wanding him.

The problem came later that night. He'd showered, changed into a clean T-shirt and boxers, and stretched out in his bunk in the CHU he shares with Dennis and Rocky. Hands locked behind his head, he closed his eyes and dropped off almost immediately.

We waited another five minutes to give him time to sink deeper. I had the wand in hand and was preparing to switch on the meter when he murmured something in his sleep. I didn't catch it, but his next mutter was clear. Too clear.

"Oh, yeah, baby. *Yeah.*"

When he followed that with a low, guttural groan, I backed away, like fast! I'd plucked cactus needles out of his rear but wanding him during an obviously erotic dream went well beyond the call of duty.

"That's it," I told the others. "We're shutting this test down."

We got out of there fast. None of us said anything to Noel the next morning, although he asked about the test a couple of times. I palmed him off with a vague reference to inconclusive results.

Given those skewed results, Rocky was all for shipping the Sniffometer back to its inventor. I had him hold off. I wanted to study the specs more, possibly give the thing another shot. Consequently, it went into hold status along with the NLOS system.

WE'D been following news reports of the shooting incident throughout our stay at the test site. Our satellite dish sucked in TV broadcasts from around the world. Diane Roth didn't make the news in Bora-Bora or Cape Town, but she became queen of the airwaves in El Paso and environs.

Her role varied considerably from story to story. As the target of a rejected lover, she formed the central figure in a number of reports of deranged individuals who obsessed over and stalked their victims. As a single working mother, she won praise from women's groups and condemnation from a few ultra-right-wing conservatives who thought she should stay home with her kids.

But it was her role as the iron-nerved heroine who prevented possible injury or death to innocent bystanders that earned her the keys to the city toward the end of our stay at the site.

My team and I crammed into the D-FAC to watch the coverage on the six o'clock news. The ceremony had taken place earlier that afternoon in the mayor's office. Diane looked sharp in her Class A greens, with the campaign ribbons she'd earned during her overseas tours on her chest.

When the camera zoomed in to highlight her cap of shining blond hair and brilliant smile, Noel sat up straighter and instinctively flexed his muscles.

"That's the gal who took down the shooter?"

"That's her," I confirmed.

"Wow!"

The rest of us avoided looking at him. And each other, until the camera panned to two equally blond youngsters.

"Cute kids," O'Reilly commented. "Hey, Techno Diva! Isn't that Mitch?"

"Where?"

"Standing next to the woman with gray hair?"

I caught only a glimpse of him before the camera moved on but there was no mistaking Jeff Mitchell's sun-streaked tawny hair and square jaw.

"Yeah, it is. Diane—Sergeant Roth—must have invited him to the ceremony. She said her kids had really taken a shine to him."

Funny Mitch hadn't mentioned being invited to the ceremony last time we talked. 'Course, this key-to-the-city thing could have been set up in a hurry. I suspected the mayor's staff had waited until the police completed their investigation, then rushed to get their boss some face time with the heroine of the moment.

Mitch confirmed my guess when he called during our last afternoon on-site. I was in the admin side of the lab, reviewing our post-test reports before the team boxed everything up. As always, the mere sound of Mitch's voice generated a little tingle of pleasure.

"I saw you on TV the other night, big guy."

"You did, huh?"

"Yep. Right there in the mayor's office with Diane and Trish and Joey."

"It was a last-minute kind of thing. She called that morning, said the kids had asked if I could come."

"Sounds like you made quite an impression on them."

"It's more the other way around. Joey's a lively one, but Trish is a real sweetie. She reminds me of Jenny when she was that age."

The pause before he said his daughter's name was so slight anyone else might have missed it. Hurting for him, I confirmed that we intended to close down the site by noon tomorrow and be back in town by early evening.

"I would be waiting to welcome you home, but I switched shifts to make the cookout on Saturday. You still up for that?"

"Am I up for red meat and beer? After ten days of Pen's herbal tea, organic grains, and soy steaks, with only the occasional trip to Pancho's for tequila and green chili stew? What do you think?"

His chuckle eased some of the ache I felt for him. I hoped it eased his, too.

"Diane said she'd fire up the grill at noon," he told me. "I should finish debrief by eight or eight thirty that morning, so I'll run home, grab a quick shower, and swing by to pick you up on the way."

"I have a better idea. Why don't you bring a change of clothes and shower at my place?" I dropped my voice a couple octaves and treated him to my best imitation of sultry, smokey Eartha Kitt. "I'll give you a free back scrub, fella."

"Sounds like a plan."

The smile was back in his voice. So was the tingle in my veins. When we disconnected, I threw a glance over my shoulder and saw the rest of the gang was otherwise occupied. Just for kicks, I slid the Sniffometer out of its case and flipped the switch.

I didn't rank up there with Sergeant Cassidy on the sexual arousal scale, but the needle was definitely headed in the right direction. Grinning in anticipation, I slipped the meter back into its case.

FST-3 has worked together long enough to devise a quick, all-encompassing routine for powering up and shutting down our test site.

We finished drafting the last of our test reports by noon. After lunch we pulled out our individual checklists. Rocky, Pen, and I re-crated the items we hadn't already shipped back to their owners and loaded equipment into the van. Dennis had kitchen duty. He emptied the fridge, bundled up our trash, and hauled all disposables to the Dumpster.

Noel is our power guy. He disconnected the satellite dish, stored it inside the D-FAC, and shut off power to all CHUs except the lab. That had to be kept at an even temperature to maintain the equipment stored there. The ATVs went into the storage shed, the spare gasoline cans into Noel's pickup to be refilled for our next deployment to Dry Springs.

Once we'd loaded our personal gear, we padlocked the storage shed and the CHUs and hit the road. Pen rode shotgun in the convertible again. I'd put the top down, but she didn't seem to mind the wind. Of course, we had to make a stop at Pancho's, where I gave its proprietor the mandatory peck on the cheek. Pen rose up on her Birkenstocked toes and did the same.

I'm a little slow in the nuance department at times. Just ask my mother. Or my ex. Or any in my string of long-suffering supervisors. They'll tell you subtlety is lost on me. That's my only excuse for taking so long to ID the rosy hue that colored Pen's cheeks when she dropped back on her heels.

It dawned on me after we'd hit the road. That was a blush. Sturdy, no-nonsense Pen, who hadn't moved the Sniffometer more than a few ticks off center, had *blushed*!

Okay, I had to know.

"What's with the heat that rushed into your cheeks when you kissed Pancho?" I asked. "Is there something going on between you two?"

"Not yet. I'm considering it, however."

My jaw dropped. Literally and figuratively. I swear I heard it thud against my chest.

Pen caught my fish face and smiled. "Don't look so surprised, Samantha. He's a very attractive man."

"He's also married. To more than one woman, if the rumors are true."

"Yes, well, there is that to consider," she said with unruffled calm. "Mitch could help us there. You are seeing him this weekend, aren't you? Maybe he could make a few calls to his contacts on the other side of the border."

"Maybe," I said, grappling with the idea of sturdy, earth-mother Pen and one-eyed Pancho. Together. In bed.

I was still struggling with the whole idea when Mitch showed up at my place early Saturday morning.

I'd spent the previous evening deleting several dozen calls from reporters from my answering machine, doing laundry, and perusing the glamour magazines that had stacked up in the mailbox during my absence. When Mitch arrived, he delivered a welcome-home kiss that left us both breathing *very* hard and brought me—eventually—to the astounding developments out in Dry Springs.

"You'll never guess what Pen laid on me yesterday," I said as he dropped his change of clothes over the back of the sofa. "She's got a thing for Pancho."

"Pen?" His brows soared under his floppy brimmed boonie hat. "And *Pancho*?"

"I know, I know! I can't believe it, either."

"Well," he said slowly, scraping a hand across his jaw. "I guess it makes sense. She's brilliant. He's shrewder than he likes to let on. She's got her, er, quirks. He's definitely got his. She's single. He's . . ."

"Not," I finished. "Rumor has it he has at least one wife, maybe more, in Mexico."

"You don't know that for a fact."

"No, I don't. But I'd like to. So would Pen. Think you could make some calls for her? Tap your contacts on the other side of the border? Separate fact from fiction?"

"You asking me to exploit my Border Patrol connections for personal reasons?"

"Yes."

He hooked a hand in the waist of my cutoffs and tugged me closer. My pulse stuttered and damned near stopped as a smile crept into his gold-flecked hazel eyes.

"What's it worth to you, woman?"

I pursed my lips and gave the matter serious consideration. "I've already offered to scrub your back. How about I include the front?"

"Done."

Anticipation shooting to every extremity, I led the way into the bedroom. We shucked our clothes as we went. I'd spent the morning in cutoffs, a tank top, and flip-flops. Mitch had come directly from work, so he had more to shuck than I did. Consequently, I was ready first and had staked out my portion of the glassed-in shower stall while he was still shedding his boots and uniform pants.

When he joined me, my already racing pulse kicked into overdrive. In the months we'd been seeing each other I'd come to know the planes and contours of his strong, muscled body. Yet the sight of it never failed to stir those primordial urges that drive the female of every species.

My ex had stirred the same atavistic urges. We'd been so hungry for each other those first few dates, so sure we'd met our match that we surfaced from a particularly wild session between the sheets and headed straight for Vegas's Little White Chapel Tunnel of Love Drive Thru.

I'd reminded myself of that hormone-driven insanity regularly in the months following our divorce. I used to chant Charlie's name like a mantra whenever I felt the sap rising, so to speak.

I'd chanted it *a lot* when I'd first met Mitch. Didn't help. Heat sizzled between us from day one. It still sizzles, jumping from nerve ending to nerve ending like electrical sparks. All I had to do was let my gaze roam his broad chest and flat belly to feel my own stomach clench in eager anticipation. His lazy smile when he handed me the soap and a washcloth only added to the zing.

"Okay, Spade." He leaned his shoulders against the slick tiles. "Do your worst."

My worst turned out to be pretty darn close to my all-time best. It was so good we had to abruptly abandon the shower and take to the bed. We left wet tracks, wet towels, wet everything in our urgent need to get horizontal.

WHEN we finished I lay sprawled across Mitch, boneless with pleasure. I didn't have the energy to raise my head, much less get dressed and drive to a cookout.

"You sure you want to go over to Diane's?" I mumbled into a mat of soft, springy chest hair.

"Too late to renege now."

"I guess."

"We'd better move it. I told her we'd bring drinks and deli potato salad."

I tried to analyze my reluctance as I put myself back together again. I finally boiled it down to the hollowness I'd glimpsed in Mitch's eyes when he'd watched Diane's kids. I knew how much he missed his own daughter. It had to drive the knife in deeper to be around a little girl who reminded him of Jenny at that age.

Or not. Maybe I was completely off base here. Maybe a few hours spent with Diane's children eased the ache. If that was the case, I vowed, the kids were about to inherit an honorary and very doting auntie.

CHAPTER SEVEN

MITCH and I drove our separate cars to Diane's place. He needed sleep after his long shift—and early morning workout! So we agreed he would head home when we left Diane's. Along the way we stopped at the deli for potato salad, beer, and soft drinks.

By the time we arrived for the cookout, the noon sun had nudged the temperature up to the mid-seventies. Perfect for my jeans and purple paisley tank, although Mitch had opted for more conservative khakis and a hunter green polo shirt embroidered with the U.S. Border Patrol insignia.

Joey and Trish had obviously been watching for us. When we parked at the curb in front of Diane's apartment, they burst out the front door and charged down the sidewalk.

"Mr. Mitch! Mr. Mitch!"

Grinning, he scooped them up and carried them back inside, one under each arm. I followed with the drinks and potato salad. Diane waited at the door, also in jeans and a stretchy top in bright poppy. She'd traded the white gauze pad and tape for two small, skin colored bandages over the deepest cuts. The rest showed only as small nicks and bruises on her skin.

"Hi, Mitch. Hi, Lieutenant."

I started to tell her to call me Samantha but let it slide. God knows I'm fuzzy around the edges when it comes to military protocol. I probably breach or bend the rules a dozen times a day. Yet I've discovered this rank thing hangs over us military types even when we're off duty and out of uniform.

"Thanks for bringing the salad and drinks. I've set everything up out back. Hope you don't mind," she said as she led the way through the apartment to a set of sliding glass doors, "but I've invited Annette Hall. She takes care of the kids when I'm pulling shifts. You met her, Mitch, at the mayor's office."

"I remember."

"She called a few minutes ago to say she's just finishing up the coleslaw and will be here shortly."

The glass doors gave onto a miniscule patio bordered by a few square yards of grass. A turtle-shaped sandbox took up one corner of the grassy area, a somewhat battered plastic castle the other. Two bright, shiny new bikes held places of honor next to the castle—a red tricycle for Joey and a blue two-wheeler with sparkly handgrips for Trish.

"They were a gift," Diane explained when the kids dragged Mitch over to admire their bikes. "From the sporting goods shop in the mall."

She hooked a strand of pale hair behind her ear and passed me a beer. We left the soft drinks for Mitch and the kids.

"You wouldn't believe all the thank-yous and gift certificates the merchants have sent me. Several people who were there during the shooting, even some complete strangers, have sent cards, too. And money."

A crease formed between her delicately penciled brows. She glanced at her children and lowered her voice.

"I won't say I can't use the cash. The gifts are great, too. I just . . . Well . . ."

"What?"

"I feel kind of mercenary to be profiting from Ollie's death."

I decided not to point out that she could refuse the gifts. As she'd indicated, she could certainly use a little help.

"Mitch told me he checked with a friend in the El Paso PD," I said instead. "The autopsy showed Austin had evidently stopped taking all his prescribed medications."

"That's what my commander told me when he reinstated me to full duty."

"So you're back on shifts?"

"Starting Tuesday. Hey, what are you doing Monday afternoon?"

"I'll be in the office, summarizing our test reports. Why?"

"One of the gift certificates I received is for a full spa and beauty treatment at Canyon Ranch. For two. If you took off, say, at noon on Monday, we could treat ourselves to the works."

Now that was a gift I wouldn't have refused, either! Canyon Ranch billed itself as the most exclusive spa in a five-state region. I'm not sure how it racks up against the high-priced health and beauty retreats in Scottsdale and Santa Fe, but I was certainly willing to give it a shot.

"You sure you don't want to take someone from work? Or maybe your neighbor?"

"Annette wouldn't enjoy it. Besides, you deserve a share of this booty. You acted as quickly and decisively as I did."

"Not hardly."

She looked at me with a question in her brown eyes. "One of the reporters told me he'd left a bunch of calls on your answering machine. They even staked out your condo. Why wouldn't you talk to the media?"

"To be honest, I didn't want to get into the details of what I was doing in that parking lot."

"Oh, that's right. You were conducting some kind of test."

She didn't ask for the specifics and I didn't volunteer them. Best to let sleeping NLOS systems lie.

"Well? Want to go all out at Canyon Ranch with me?"

"I'd love to."

"Great! Why don't I swing by your office at noon and pick you up? I'd like to see what you do. Oh, good. There's the doorbell. That should be Annette."

Joey and Trish greeted their babysitter with smiles and bear hugs. The slender, sixtyish widow returned the hugs with obvious affection. She remembered Mitch from the mayor's ceremony and said she was glad to see him again. When Diane introduced me, Hall treated me to a fierce hug, too.

"From what Diane has told me, you saved her life."

"It was more the other way around."

"Well, I think you're both remarkable women."

She claimed the folding lawn chair next to mine while Diane delivered sodas to Mitch and the kids.

"I thank my lucky stars for the day I met Diane and her children at the playground. I'd just moved to El Paso and was feeling so lonely. Taking care of Trish and Joey has put the sparkle back in my life."

"The feeling's mutual. Diane told me she didn't know how she would manage without you."

Beaming, the older woman gazed at the foursome in the yard. "She's so good with those two. So is Mitch."

"Mmmmm."

I won't say it made me uncomfortable to see the cozy, family-style tableau the four of them made, but it did stir some odd thoughts.

"Diane has had such a rough time of it. And now this shooting!" Tch-tching, Annette shook her head.

"It's been so hard on her, coming so soon after the tragic loss of her in-laws."

Surprised, I set my dew-streaked beer bottle on the table beside my chair. "They're dead?"

"Oh, dear." Annoyed with herself, the silver-haired Annette bit her lip. "I shouldn't have said anything. I just assumed Diane had told you."

"She said her in-laws had fought for custody of the children but it was all behind her now. I didn't realize she meant that literally. What happened?"

Obviously reluctant, Annette flicked a glance at the others. I didn't push. I didn't have to. She realized she'd let the cat out of the bag and continued in a hushed voice.

"From what I understand, they were bludgeoned to death by a burglar."

"Good God!"

"It happened just a few weeks before Diane was supposed to rotate back to the States. She had to get an emergency . . . uh . . . I think she called it a curtailment. Anyway, she rushed home from Afghanistan to take care of the kids."

My heart twisted. I couldn't imagine the trauma such a violent act must have caused those two children.

"What a horrible thing for Trish and Joey to go through."

"They weren't there when it happened, thank heavens. The grandparents had just dropped Trish off at school and Joey at nursery school. Diane said the police think they surprised the burglar when they returned home."

I didn't remember reading about a double homicide. "Was this here in El Paso?"

"No. They lived in Florida. Town with a funny name. Kimsee or Kissme or something like that. Joey and Trish never say it the same way twice."

"This family *has* had its share of tragedy," I murmured.

"It certainly has." Pausing, Annette thinned her lips. "I don't like to disparage the dead, but those people put Diane through hell when they tried to get custody of the children. She doesn't speak ill of them, however, which speaks well of her."

Not totally true. I distinctly recalled Sergeant Roth referring to her "bitch of a mother-in-law." I could understand the lapse, though. That was right after the shooting, when her emotions had to be as raw and as close to the surface as mine were.

Funny she hadn't mentioned her in-laws' brutal murders, though. Only that the battle for custody was over. Then again, we *were* both still pretty shaken up.

My gaze went to the cozy tableau again. No wonder the kids had latched onto Mitch—and, apparently, Annette Hall—so quickly. They'd experienced way too much turmoil and loss in their young lives.

The tableau broke up a moment later. Diane asked Mitch to fire up the grill while she went into the house for the hamburger patties. Annette pushed out of her chair and accompanied her.

"I'll help you, dear."

That left me to ease into my self-designated role as honorary auntie.

"That's really a neat castle," I commented to Trish.

"You want to get in with me?"

"I, uh, sure."

We scrunched down inside the plastic walls. I tucked my knees under my chin so Trish could let down the drawbridge for her brother to crawl in as well. I wasn't quite sure what to do next but got inspiration from the kids' shiny gold curls.

"Do you know the story of Rapunzel?"

"Isn't she the one who let down her braid like a rope so some dorky prince could climb up and rescue her?"

"You don't like that story?"

"Nuh-uh. My mom says it's dumb to sit around and wait to be rescued. She says me 'n' Joey gotta study hard in school so we kin be smart enough to care of ourselves."

Nothing like being put in your place by a seven-year-old. I glanced up, caught Mitch's grin, and nodded solemnly.

"That's very good advice."

"I know."

My would-be honorary niece gave a prissy nod. Luckily for our future relationship, she reverted to a giggly little girl in the next breath.

"I'd let down a braid for Tyler Taylor, though. He's sooo cool."

I drew a complete blank. Thankfully, no response was required as Trish launched into a nonstop monologue about a kid I eventually understood was the latest adolescent heartthrob to burst on the scene.

"Tyler's new movie is gonna be at the theater next Saturday," Trish gushed. "Mom says she'll take me if she doesn't have to work 'n' Mrs. Hall will keep Joey. I already know three of the songs by heart. Wanna hear them?"

"Okay."

She launched into a clear, high treble and never missed a beat as she went from one song right into the next. I sat there with my chin on my knees, amazed that she remembered every line of the lyrics.

Diane returned with stacked platters in time for the last verse. After we all duly applauded her daughter's performance, she sent the kids inside to wash up. A still-grinning Mitch had to reach down a hand to extricate me from the castle.

"What do you think?" I asked him. "Should I take Trish to this movie next week if Diane can't? You could entertain Joey while we're drooling over this hunk Taylor and meet us afterward."

The smile that lit his eyes was answer enough. "Sounds like a plan."

"You two don't have to give up your afternoon," our hostess protested.

"It'll be my pleasure," I said. "Besides, you're treating me to the works at Canyon Ranch. Least I can do is return the favor."

* * *

MY anticipation of an afternoon and evening of decadent indulgence at a world-class spa mounted during the following day. So did my curiosity about Diane Roth's in-laws.

Since it was a lazy Sunday, I decked out in loose-fitting gray sweats and a well-washed USAF sweatshirt, plopped down at my desk, and powered up my laptop. Didn't take long to narrow Kimsee and/or Kissme down to Kissimmee, Florida. Or search the online archives of the *Osceola News-Gazette*, which serviced that area. The brutal murder of two respected citizens in their own home had dominated the headlines for several days.

I gave a low whistle at the photos of the Roths' estate. Set on the edge of a lake, the plantation-style residence featured white columns, weathered brick, tall shutters, and a wraparound porch. Diane had mentioned her in-laws had money. Here was the black-and-white proof.

No wonder she'd had to spend most of her off-duty time in Afghanistan trying to communicate with her lawyer. Judging by the elegance of their home, the Roths could have poured megabucks into their fight for custody of their grandkids.

Chin in hand, I read through the articles. I knew they withheld many of the crime-scene details. The details they did reveal were pretty gory. The final article several weeks after the murders indicated the police had no suspect and were offering a substantial reward for any information leading to an arrest. The same article included an interview with a forensic psychologist, who suggested the brutal murders were the act of a seriously ill sociopath.

I tapped a finger on the keypad and re-read the psychologist's opinion while a nasty thought slowly strung together. Two people closely connected to Diane Roth bludgeoned to death. She herself attacked by a PTSD sufferer who'd gone off his meds. When I went to bed Sunday night, I couldn't help wondering if the perpetrator in each case could have been the same person.

THAT uneasy speculation got pushed to the back of my mind Monday morning.

My team and I had our usual start-of-the-day confab. Our main objective was to review the final draft of our test report. We agreed on most of the items but I was still disappointed over the mixed results of both the NLOS system and the Sniffometer. I insisted both systems warranted further testing and spent the morning writing up justification for follow-on tests before putting my final stamp of approval on the report. I had just zinged it off to Dr. J at DARPA HQ when Sergeant Cassidy escorted Diane into my cubbyhole of an office.

Surprised, I glanced at my watch. "Is it noon already?"

"Almost."

"I'm sorry. I lost track of the time. I should have been on the lookout for you and escorted you in."

Security in these thirties-era buildings isn't precisely up to Fort Knox standards, but we do try. All visitors have to have a pass and an escort. *Particularly* when those visitors are unhappy inventors whose projects we'd rejected.

"Not a problem," Noel said, his admiring gaze fixed on Diane. "I heard Sergeant Roth buzz and issued the pass."

"Thanks."

I waited a beat. Two beats. Cleared my throat.

"Thank you, Sergeant Cassidy."

"What? Oh. Yes, ma'am." His glance shot back to Diane. "Nice meeting you, Roth."

Her glance stayed locked on him. Angling her head, she followed his progress down the hall.

"Wowza! Are all those muscles for real?"

"You wouldn't ask that if you had to listen to him clanking weights for hours on end, like the rest of us do when we're out at our test site."

She looked around, curiosity stamped across her delicate features. "Just what is it you guys test?"

"Small inventions that by some wild stretch of the imagination might have military application in a desert environment."

She nodded to the NLOS goggles sitting on my desk next to the Sniffometer.

"Like those sci-fi glasses you were wearing the night of the shooting?"

"Yes."

"What are they supposed to do?"

I waved her to one of the chairs in front of my desk

and gave her a layman's explanation of omnidirectional transmitters and solar-blind ultraviolet wavelengths. Or tried to. Her face soon took on that glazed look I'm sure mine did when Rocky and Pen went technical on me.

"And that?" she asked when I gave it up as hopeless. "What's that wand thing?"

"It measures BO."

"BO? Like in body odor?"

"Yep."

"You've got to be kidding!"

"I wish. The inventor claims our body odors are as distinct as our fingerprints and precisely reflect our moods, which this little gadget then gauges."

"Does it work?"

"Sort of. Here, I'll show you." I flicked the switch on the wand and waited for the meter to reset. "Ready?"

Diane looked doubtful but struck a pose. "Ready."

I aimed the wand in her direction, waited a moment, and checked the meter.

"What does it say?"

"That you're calm and content."

"I think you just measured the new perfume one of the merchants sent me," she replied with a laugh. "It's called Tranquility."

"Glad it's working. From the sound of it, your life has been anything but tranquil lately."

"No kidding!" She blew out a long breath. "I thought I'd seen the worst in Afghanistan."

Then she came home to a double homicide. I hesitated, reluctant to mention the murders but the research I'd done last night had raised too many questions to avoid the subject.

"Annette told me about your in-laws," I said as I lowered the wand. "How tragic for them, and how awful for Trish and Joey."

The laughter drained from her eyes. "It was a nightmare. A horrible nightmare. The kids weren't there when it happened, though, for which I thank God every night."

She looked away for a moment, then brought her gaze back to me.

"I got so I hated them," she admitted in a gruff voice. "All those months in Afghanistan, when they were trying to take my kids, I hated them. Then this terrible, terrible thing happened and I hated myself for the vicious thoughts I'd had about them."

"I've had a few nasty thoughts in my time," I admitted. "Particularly where my ex is concerned."

I paused again. I didn't want to worry Diane. She had enough on her plate. Yet I couldn't shake the nagging feeling there might be more to the attempt on her life than either of us had realized.

"Has it occurred to you there might be a connection between the attack on your in-laws and the attack on you?"

She threw me a startled glance. "What?"

"Oliver Austin. Could he have tried to get back at you for rejecting him by going after the kids?"

The mere suggestion that her children might have

been the real target in that vicious attack in Florida made her nostrils flare and her breath come fast.

"No! Ollie wouldn't have done that! He . . . He couldn't!"

"Even if he was off his meds?" I asked gently. "I did some research on PTSD after the shooting. Reportedly it affects every patient differently. And you can't just quit some of the medications used to treat it. You have to come off them slowly, under a doctor's supervision."

She sat back in her chair, obviously shaken. It took a moment or two for the color to return to her cheeks.

"Ollie couldn't have attacked my in-laws. He was still in the VA hospital, undergoing medical evaluation."

"Oh. Well, that settles that."

Except . . .

Austin had been under investigation for unspecified activities. He could have been involved in anything. Had contacts or accomplices here in the States. That niggling thought was at the back of my mind as I shut off the Sniffometer and grabbed my hat and purse from my desk drawer.

"Let's blow this joint. I'm ready for some total decadence."

"So am I!"

CHAPTER EIGHT

OKAY, here it is, folks. My last wish and testament. When I keel over and drop dead while testing some off-the-wall gizmo, I want to go to Canyon Ranch Heaven.

Just the approach to the exclusive spa was enough to cause heart palpitations. We drove up in Diane's rental, as her Tahoe was in the repair shop after being released from the police impound lot. One glimpse, and we were both straining against our seat belts to take in the unfolding splendor.

As its name implies, the spa sat nestled in a canyon formed by a spur of the Franklin Mountains. The curving drive leading up to it was marked by boulders engraved with Anasazi designs. Rain dancers, coyotes, spirals, and lightning bolts led the way to a flat-roofed adobe complex in a glowing shade of ochre. A uniformed valet greeted us at an entrance shaded by a wooden portico spilling huge clusters of purple wisteria.

"Welcome to Canyon Ranch. May I have your names so I can alert your personal attendants of your arrival?"

Diane and I exchanged glances. Personal attendants, no less. Waggling her brows, she supplied the information.

"Sergeant Diane Roth and Lieutenant Samantha Spade."

"Please go in, ladies."

The receptionist came out from behind her desk and greeted us with cups of pale yellow tea. I braced myself, but this fragrant blend didn't pack anywhere near the same obnoxious wallop as Pen's herbal infusions.

Our mauve-robed attendants arrived before Diane and I had taken little more than a sip or two. One was a tall, willowy redhead with a name tag that identified her as Susannah. The other was an equally willowy brunette named Jon. I won't say he minced across the tile floor. He came darn close, though.

"Sergeant Roth!" Gripping Diane's hand with both of his, he gushed all over her. "I'm so honored to meet you. I've been following the news reports of that terrible incident. You were so brave."

"Not really." She eased free of his grip. "Just trained to react in an emergency situation. Lieutenant Spade was there, too. She put herself at risk to warn the rest of us."

It was my turn for a two-handed squeeze.

"I think you're both incredibly brave." Jon shuddered dramatically. "I couldn't imagine what I would do in a similar situation."

The guy's grip was surprisingly strong. He might be able to take down an attacker if he had his back to the wall.

After Susannah introduced herself, the two attendants led us through a set of bronze doors into a wide, airy forecourt illuminated by skylights and fragrant with the scent of vanilla. Susannah swept two embossed folders off a marble counter.

"We've prepared a suggested agenda based on the services you indicated you might be interested in when you made the reservation, Sergeant Roth. Or may I call you Diane?"

"Diane, please."

"And I'm Samantha."

Nodding, she handed us the folders. "There's a complete list of all our services in the changing rooms. If you see anything you'd like to add to the agenda we've prepared, just say the word."

"Will do."

"You're in room three, Samantha. Diane, we've put you in four. You'll find robes and shower shoes in each. Jon and I will wait for you here. Take your time," she added with a smile. "We're at your complete disposal for the rest of the day."

Diane and I headed for our assigned rooms. Mine was larger than the living room in my apartment. More elegant, too, unless you're really into shabby chic. Curious, I flipped open the embossed folder and skimmed the agenda. It looked good. *Very* good. Until I compared it to the list of services in the bound book set on a table next to a pitcher of water with floating lemons.

Holy crapola! Three hundred dollars for a seaweed wrap? Two-fifty for a hot sand pumice? I could go out and roll around in the desert for nothing!

Gulping, I knocked on the connecting door to Diane's room. When she poked her head through the opening, I held up the price list.

"Have you looked at this?"

One glance, and she was as shell-shocked as I was.

"Good Lord!"

"You're sure our sessions are free?"

"That's what they said. Let me double-check."

She was back a few moments later.

"Yep, it's all free."

I took my lower lip between my teeth and almost made a meal of it. My gut told me I shouldn't do this. Very belatedly, I'll admit. What can I say? I'm a lieutenant. Even with that excuse, I'm embarrassed to confess I might not have thought twice if not for those exorbitant prices.

They reminded me forcibly that DARPA follows the Department of Defense's strict guidelines vis-à-vis dealings with contractors. We're not supposed to accept a free lunch or cup of coffee from individuals or firms doing, or seeking to do, business with the military. As far as I knew, this high-priced spa wasn't angling for a contract with any of the military units in this region. Still . . .

"I'm having second thoughts about this, Diane."

"Why?"

"My team and I conduct tests that could result in lucrative contracts to both businesses and private individuals. I probably shouldn't accept free services. It could be construed as a conflict of interest."

"I don't see how, unless you guys test spa products and services."

"Actually, we *have* tested some far-out creams and lotions. And," I added as I thought more about it, "I know of at least one antiaging cream on the market today that began life as a DARPA-funded research project. They were trying to synthesize human elastin to speed the healing of war wounds and reduce scarring."

Lips pursed, she considered that for a moment. "I see what you're saying. But *I'm* not in a position to offer anyone a lucrative contract."

"True. Tell you what. You go ahead and enjoy yourself. I'll call one of my team and ask them to come get me."

"Hang on a sec. Let's talk about this."

Frowning, she came into my changing room and hitched a hip against a counter arrayed with stacked towels, a neatly folded robe, and slippers.

"I think you may be overreacting. These merchants just want to thank me—thank both of us—for preventing what could have been a bloodbath."

"I know. But the major at our headquarters who got fired for letting a private think tank reimburse him for travel expenses probably thought they just wanted to thank him, too." I gave the fluffy, stacked towels a glance of real longing. "I sure hate to miss out on all this, but . . ."

"So stay. Get detoxed. Be pumiced."

"You stay. I'm going to pass, Diane."

Her frown deepened. On Trish or Joey, it would be considered a sulk. "You want to tell me how I'm supposed to enjoy myself after you've laid on this massive guilt trip?"

"I'm sorry. That wasn't my intention."

"Yeah, well, that's the result." Still sulking, she pushed away from the counter. "I'll get my purse and we'll go."

Susannah and Jon expressed massive disappointment at our abrupt about-face and tried to convince us to reschedule. I declined. Diane said she would call them. Maybe.

A different air permeated the rental car during our drive back to Fort Bliss. Not cold, but definitely chilly. It warmed a little when Diane pulled up outside the building that housed my office.

"I'm sorry about this," I said as I reached for the door handle. "I should have thought it through when you first suggested going to the spa."

"That's okay. I'm disappointed, but I'll get over it." She hesitated, her wrists looped over the steering wheel. "You mentioned taking Trish to the opening of the new Tyler Taylor movie if I couldn't. Turns out I can't, but I'll understand if you'd rather back out of this deal, too."

"No, really. I'd love to take her."

I might have been overstating the case a bit. Miss

Trish and I hadn't exactly hit it off. Too late to back out now, though.

"The movie complex sent me a hundred-dollar gift certificate," Diane said with a rueful smile. "I won't ask if you want to use it."

"This will be my treat. I'll call you later in the week to confirm the time."

PEN, Rocky, and Dennis O'Reilly expressed surprise at seeing me back after I'd told them I was leaving for the day. Sergeant Cassidy expressed extreme disappointment that Diane Roth hadn't accompanied me inside for another visit.

I have to admit to mixed feelings as I entered my office cubicle. Part of me said I'd done the right thing by refusing such an expensive gratuity. Another part sneered and warned that I'd gone over to the dark side. A strange, dangerous place fraught with so many rules and regulations that I'd never find my way into the light again.

What the heck happened to the old Samantha? The reckless, I'll-jump-in-first girl? The laughing, flirty cocktail waitress who grabbed life with greedy hands?

The Air Force, I concluded glumly. That's what happened. Responsibility. Authority. The burdens of leadership. Mourning for my lost self, I thumped my hat and purse on my desk.

I was in no mood to fiddle around with more test reports. Or the equipment I'd left lying on my desk. I started to shove the items aside, but the thin paper printout hanging from one like a tail snagged my attention.

Frowning, I called over the partitions. "Hey! Who's been playing with the Sniffometer?"

Pen scooted her desk chair back and stuck her head around the divider between our offices. "No one. Why?"

"The reading on this printout is all over the place."

"Weren't you demonstrating it to Sergeant Roth before you left?"

"Oh. Right."

Pen scooted back to her desk. I sank down at mine and studied the wild zigs and zags on the printout. According to the Olfactory Somatosensory Indicator, Diane's odor emissions during her short visit to my office had swung from a median level of calm to extreme agitation to fear.

Well, hell! Now I felt like a total jerk. Not only had I ruined her day at the spa, I'd had to bring up that business about her in-laws' murder. Worse, I'd posed the possibility of a link to Oliver Austin. Even theorized he might have been trying to get to her through her children.

I'd seen the evidence of Diane's physical reaction to that theory firsthand. I didn't need the Sniffometer to verify the mere idea had scared the living crap out of her.

I might have let the whole thing drop right there if the last, small segment of the printout hadn't registered odor emissions strongly suggestive of untruthfulness.

Forehead scrunched, I tried to reconstruct our conversation. What would she have lied about? Wishing evil on her in-laws? Feeling guilty about that? Insisting Austin wasn't capable of such a vicious act?

Maybe he wasn't, but he might have associated with others who were. Special Agent Blue Eyes from CID headquarters said the man was being investigated for unspecified activities while in Afghanistan.

My fertile and admittedly overactive imagination took off. Chin in hand, I stared at that damned printout and formulated all kinds of wild theories.

What if Austin had been so bitter about Roth's rejection he decided on revenge before he rotated back to the States? Or maybe while he was in the VA hospital. He could have conspired with an equally sick or possibly a criminal accomplice to go after her kids. And when that didn't work, he came after her himself.

I didn't have a shred of proof linking Austin or a cohort to the murders in Kissimmee, Florida. But I did have a very sexy law enforcement sweetie to bounce these uneasy thoughts off.

UNFORTUNATELY, my law enforcement sweetie wasn't available for consultation. I got the word when I checked the messages on my answering machine after work that evening.

"Hey, Samantha. This is Mitch. I didn't want to disturb you at the spa. I figured you were wallowing in mud or wrapped in seaweed with cucumbers plastered all over your face."

I wish!

"Just wanted to let you know I'm jumping a plane for San Diego in an hour. I got tagged to work a task force evaluating the president's initiative to prevent Mexico's drug wars from spilling across our borders. Don't know how long this is going to take. Guess I'll see you when I see you."

Guess so.

I called in a delivery order at Ding How, my favorite Chinese restaurant. I've gotten hooked on their fiery General Tsao's chicken. It's flavored with a sauce that tastes suspiciously similar to extra hot chili sauce. What can I say? They do Chinese different here in West Texas. Actually, now that I think about it, they do just about everything different in West Texas.

While waiting for supper I changed into my usual at-home attire of comfortable sweats. Then I shuffled around the apartment looking for Special Agent Blue Eyes's business card. Took me a while to find it. I remembered transferring it from my uniform pocket to my briefcase before we'd left the test site. From there it had leaped between the pages of *Elle*, where I'd evidently used it to bookmark an article on spring fashion trends. In case you're wondering, amethyst and celery are the season's hot new colors.

The doorbell rang while I was finishing the article. I laid the card on my coffee table and went to pay for the delivery. The card sat there while I chopsticked chicken from the carton and entertained serious second thoughts about contacting Agent Blue Eyes.

I'd skated on any fallout from deploying the NLOS

system the night of the shooting. Now I was getting all worked up over the unverified results of another quasi-test, also conducted under uncontrolled conditions.

Besides, what did the results indicate? Only that Diane reacted with justifiable surprise and fear at my suggestion the attacks on her and on her in-laws might be connected. And maybe shaded the truth about something.

If I had to bet, I'd put my money on that bit about hating herself for hating the Roths. She would have to be a whole lot more forgiving than the rest of us ordinary mortals to *not* be pissed at someone who was trying to take away her kids.

The chopsticks halted inches from my mouth. I sat there frozen, a chunk of spicy chicken hovering in the air as a really nasty thought boomeranged inside my head.

What if . . . ? What if Diane was so pissed, this Austin guy thought he'd do her a favor? Like arrange for someone to take out the in-laws. Get them off her back once and for all. Become Diane's instant hero, then go all vengeful when she wasn't properly appreciative.

No! I shook my head and almost stabbed myself with the chopsticks in the process. No way! If Austin had so much as hinted at a vicious plan like that, Diane would have gone straight to the authorities.

Wouldn't she?

The fact that my churning brain cells even *formulated* that thought shocked the heck out of me. It also made me feel distinctly queasy. I lowered the chopsticks and dropped the chunk of chicken back in the carton.

An image of the Roths' elegant lakeside home leaped into my mind. They'd had money. Lots of money. And I remembered Diane mentioning that Trish and Joey were their only grandchildren. So who inherited their estate?

Not the kids. If they had, Diane wouldn't be struggling to make ends meet. Unless the Roths had set up some sort of trust that the kids couldn't tap into until they came of age.

Okay, now I was getting ridiculous! In the space of a half a carton of General Tsao's chicken, Diane had gone from being a heroine to a potential beneficiary who would benefit from her in-laws' brutal murders.

Disgusted with myself, I dumped the remains of my dinner into the garbage disposal and flipped the switch. I should have ground up Agent Blue Eyes's card along with the chicken and brown rice. The damned thing was the last thing I saw before hitting the sack later that night. It was still there when I swooped my purse off the coffee table the next morning on my way to work. I stood there, debating long and hard, before stuffing the card into my purse.

I waited until after my regular morning confab with my team to make the call. As usual, they all crammed into my cubbyhole of an office. Pen with her tea and two pencils projecting from her head like antennae, Dennis O'Reilly in his perpetually wrinkled Dockers and plastic pocket pack, Sergeant Cassidy in ABUs like me.

Rocky is the only one among us who tries to dress

as a professional. Sadly, his sartorial choices don't reflect his engineering brilliance. The green paisley sport coat and pencil-thin black tie he'd donned this morning only emphasized his nervous personality.

I'd put the Sniffometer back in its case but it was still there, sitting on my credenza beside the NLOS system. I knew darn well that if I switched the thing on now and wanded myself, it would show my major histocompatibility complex was emitting a full spectrum of sensory indicators. Everything from doubt to denial to guilt for even *thinking* Diane could be in any way involved in the death of her in-laws.

"Are you with us, oh Queen of the Quacks?"

"Huh?"

Dennis nudged his glasses up with a pudgy finger and gave a long—and totally sarcastic—sigh.

"We have to send our final field test report to Dr. J by Friday. We've all provided you our input. Do you need anything else?"

"No, I'm good. I'll finish my summary this morning and zap it to you guys for a final look-see before the report goes forward."

First, however, I had to make a phone call. To steel myself for what loomed in my mind as an act of betrayal, I surreptitiously dumped my tea and snuck down the hall for a cup of coffee. The java provided the jolt I needed to place a call to CID headquarters.

"I'd like to speak to Special Agent Richard Sinclair, please."

"Who's calling?"

"Lieutenant Samantha Spade."

"May I tell Agent Sinclair what this call is in reference to?"

"The Oliver Austin investigation."

Blue Eyes came on the line a few moments later. I expected at least a hello. What I got was a terse question.

"Are you on a secure line?"

"No."

"Hang up, go to the CID detachment on post, and call me back."

CHAPTER NINE

WONDERING what the heck I'd gotten myself into, I cranked up the Sebring and drove to the CID detachment. Comb-Over Guy wasn't there (thankfully!) but one of his fellow agents was on the watch for me.

She met me at the door and took me straight back to the detachment commander's office. He gave me a strange look, then vacated his office so I could use his direct line to CID headquarters. The ensuing conversation was almost completely one-sided.

I talked, Agent Sinclair listened.

I stopped, he remained silent.

I cleared my throat, he asked for the name and phone number of my supervisor.

I gulped. "Why do you need that information?"

"Because I want you in my office ASAP. I'll talk to your boss to make sure it happens."

It happened.

Less than five minutes later, Sinclair called back and said he'd just arranged an e-ticket for a 12:20 p.m. Delta Air Lines flight. I could print out the boarding pass there at the detachment. He also informed me a rental car would be waiting when I arrived in D.C. and I was to drive straight to CID headquarters at Fort Belvoir, Virginia.

"But . . ." As far as I knew, there weren't any direct flights. "Given at least one stopover and the time differential, I won't land before eight or nine tonight."

"I'll be waiting. Your boss wants to see you, too. We set up a meeting with him tomorrow. I'll brief you on what you can and can't tell him."

Hooo-boy. A session with Dr. J. Just what I needed to cap off a hurried jaunt back East.

I hung up with the distinct feeling I'd jumped in way over my head. But into what? I wished to heck I knew!

I left the detachment with boarding pass in hand and less than two hours to rush back to my apartment, change into my service uniform, throw some things in an overnight bag, and heavy-foot it to the airport.

I called my office on the way to my apartment. My team has come to expect the unexpected these days, but this abrupt departure for Washington took them by as much surprise as it had me. Mentally crossing my fingers, I left Rocky in charge.

I had to scramble to put my service dress uniform

together. I don't wear the dark blue jacket, slacks, and light blue blouse all that often. I fixed the U.S. insignias on the collar tabs okay and centered the nickel-plated name tag. My skimpy, single row of ribbons gave me grief but I finally got it straight and pinned my DARPA badge right above. Cramming my feet into low-heeled black pumps and my flight cap with its shiny gold lieutenant's bar over my clipped-up French braid, I grabbed my purse and the overnighter and hit the door running.

I made it to the airport and through security with all of ten minutes to spare. Just long enough to grab a burrito and Coke on my way to the gate. The burrito was Tex-Mex at its best. Loaded with onions and super-hot chili sauce. Tasted fabulous going down. Not so good as I tried to smother burps all the way across country.

The Delta flight made a short stop in Houston and landed at Reagan National at 7:10. It was already dark. And chilly! February in D.C. is considerably colder than in El Paso. Wishing I'd thought to bring my Air Force overcoat, I shivered my way across the street and up the parking ramp to the rental car section.

Agent Blue Eyes had reserved a compact sedan in my name. Pretty boring after my sporty Sebring convertible, but its heater worked very nicely. Now all I had to do was battle my way south to Fort Belvoir.

I've only been to D.C. three times. Once with my high school pom squad to march in the capital's Fourth of July parade, twice to visit DARPA headquarters. Each time I'd gazed in awe at the monuments and gawked at the bumper-to-bumper gridlock otherwise known as rush hour. To my infinite relief, I caught the tail end of the mass exodus out of the city. I moved along at a decent clip while the NAVSTAR directional system in the rental sang out directions.

Once past the Beltway, the suburban sprawl of shopping malls, office buildings, and town house complexes thinned out. I drove through rolling Virginia hills studded with centuries-old oaks lifting still-leafless branches to the night sky. This was tobacco country, or used to be back in the days when huge plantations dominated historic Fairfax and Prince William counties.

I flashed my AF ID at the visitors' entrance to Fort Belvoir, but still had to go inside and get a temporary pass for the rental. The center boasted a gallery of framed photos showing the post's evolution from a pre-WWI training camp for Army engineers to its current role as a major military complex. Anxious to get to my destination, I gave the pictorial display only a cursory look-see.

After fixing the pass to my windshield, I circled a moonlit golf course and promptly got lost in the maze of facilities that comprise the South Post. I finally pulled into a huge parking lot across the street from several floodlit brick buildings. A boldly lettered sign indicated one of the buildings housed JPPSOWA, whatever that was.

Another sign announced the home of the Institute of Heraldry. For those of you who don't know, the institute has to put their chop on all the badges and insignia worn by the U.S. military. *I* know this because my team and I designed a patch for FST-3. We thought it was pretty cool and descriptive of our mission. It featured one of the items we'd tested—an ergonomic exoskeleton—wearing an Air Force flight cap, a Good Conduct Medal, and a diabolical smirk. The institute disapproved of it. In somewhat less than polite terms, I might add.

I directed a disdainful sniff at the institute and hurried up the walk leading to CID headquarters. Like the other buildings, this one was redbrick with white pillars framing the door. Legacy of the area's southern heritage, I surmised as I buzzed for entry. I had to pass through two security checkpoints and clip on a badge encoded with my digitized image before Special Agent Sinclair showed up to escort me to the inner sanctum.

"Sorry for pulling you in with such short notice, Lieutenant."

"Not a problem."

Sinclair was as short and tough as I remembered from our meeting out at the test site, with the same electric blue eyes. Only now they were rimmed with red and his formerly crisp khakis sported almost as many wrinkles as O'Reilly's.

"What's this all about?" I asked, unable to contain my curiosity.

"Let's go to the conference room. We'll brief you there."

We? I tasted spicy burrito again. Whatever I'd gotten involved in was obviously big.

Even this late in the evening, CID headquarters

hummed with activity. Not surprising, I guess, for an agency charged with investigating fraud, computer crimes, and other criminal activity worldwide as well as providing protective services for VIPs who decide to jaunt around to hot spots like Iraq and Afghanistan.

Blue Eyes led me past a brightly lit operations center crammed with computer consoles and a wall full of digital clocks showing the time in dozens of different time zones. I got an eyeful before we turned a corner and my escort pushed open a door.

"In here."

I entered a small conference room containing only a table, black vinyl chairs, and three unsmiling strangers. On the table lay an assortment of printed newspaper articles. The headlines on one caught my instant attention. Would've been hard to miss. In two-inch letters, it shouted about a "Local Couple Bludgeoned to Death." Gulping, I tore my gaze from the headlines while Sinclair made the intros.

"Lieutenant Spade, this is Agent Angela O'Donnell from our ELINT division; Agent Travis MacIntire, who runs our Afghanistan desk, and Tom Devonshire, the State Department's rep to the president's Interagency Counter-narcotics Task Force."

Electronic intelligence? Counter-narcotics?

Feeling as though I'd just stepped onto very treacherous ground, I shook hands with a brisk, businesslike O'Donnell, a thin, almost cadaverous MacIntire, and Devonshire, who looked like he hadn't slept or shaved in weeks.

"Care for some coffee before we get started?" Blue Eyes asked.

"Yes, please."

I knew I would need the jolt. If the grim expressions on these characters' faces were any indication, this was going to be a terse session.

"All right," Sinclair said when I was duly supplied with a cup of tarry liquid, "please tell the others what you told me. Specifically, why you think Oliver Austin was connected to the murder of Sergeant Diane Roth's in-laws."

"I didn't say he *was* connected. I said I thought he could be."

"Why?"

I hesitated, my hands wrapped around the ceramic mug. "You informed them this is all sheer supposition on my part, didn't you?"

"I did."

I shot a glance around the table. Looking at those un-smiling and haggard faces, I came close—*very* close—to wishing I'd kept my mouth shut. Downing a swig of a brew almost as noxious as Pen's herbal infusions, I started with the shooting.

"Diane told the police responding to the shooting in-cident that she'd been stationed with Austin in Afghani-stan. She said they hung out together occasionally." I hesitated a moment. "She didn't say so, but I got the impression they might have been more than friends."

"They were," Blue Eyes confirmed. "When we inter-viewed her, she admitted to a short but intense affair."

"That's how she described Austin to the police. Very intense. Too intense for her. She was relieved when he rotated back to the States some months before she did and didn't reply to his subsequent emails."

Sinclair kept his expression carefully neutral, but I saw O'Donnell drop her gaze to hide a sudden flicker in her eyes. Which told me Diana *had*, in fact, responded to Austin's emails.

A queasy feeling stirred in the pit of my stomach.

"What else did Sergeant Roth tell you about Oliver Austin?"

"Just what she told the police. That she didn't learn he'd been diagnosed with PTSD and subsequently separated from the Army until she got back to the States. She said she called the VA hospital where he was being treated, but he'd checked himself out and disappeared. She hadn't had any contact with him at all until he showed up in El Paso and started shooting."

No flicker in O'Donnell's eyes—or anyone else's—this time.

"So what did Sergeant Roth say," Sinclair continued, his piercing gaze locked on my face, "that made you think Oliver Austin might have been involved in the deaths of Helen and Peter Roth?"

"Diane didn't say anything. In fact, she didn't even tell me that her in-laws had been murdered. I heard about it from her neighbor, who babysits her kids. But Diane *did* tell me the Roths had tried to get custody of their grandchildren. She'd had to fight them the whole time she was deployed. So I thought . . . I wondered . . ."

"What?"

"If Austin had become obsessed with her, he might have thought he could help by getting rid of her most pressing fear—losing her children."

"And you raised this possibility with Diane?"

"I did, but she said he was still in the VA hospital when the murders happened."

Sinclair leaned forward, his elbows bent and his hands locked on the table. "Until your phone call this morning, we had no knowledge of the Florida murders. The Kissimmee police investigated the crime. They didn't notify us, as there was no connection to the military, other than the fact the Roths were taking care of their grandchildren while their mother served overseas. We've since learned that the Roths didn't advertise the fact they were suing for custody of their grandchildren, so it never figured as a factor in the investigation."

"I can understand why they would keep it quiet," I said around the lump that seemed to have taken up permanent residence in my throat. "Might not play well in the local papers to be going after a single mom serving in a combat zone. Especially after agreeing to take care of her kids while she was deployed."

Agent O'Donnell spoke up for the first time. "The custody petition had to be filed in the children's legal state of residence. Sergeant Roth was stationed at Fort Stewart, Georgia, before she deployed. She gave her in-laws a conditional power of attorney to act on certain matters concerning the children's health and welfare, but she maintained Georgia as her—and her kids'—

residence of record. From what we've uncovered in the past six hours, all legal work concerning the custody suit was handled by a Georgia attorney the Roths hired."

"What about . . . ?" I hated myself for asking, hated the ugly suspicions I'd raised. "What about the Roths' estate? Diane said they had money. Lots of money. Do you know who inherited?"

"The will is still tied up in probate, but the Kissimmee PD investigator we talked to indicates half the estate goes to various charities. The other half is divided equally between their only living issue—the two grandchildren."

Oh, Lord! Talk about motive!

"But," Sinclair continued as I writhed internally, "aside from a small cash settlement when they graduate from high school and stipulations to cover college costs, the principal would be held in trust until they reach twenty-five."

So the kids wouldn't benefit from their grandparents' death for several decades. Did Diane have prior knowledge of that? I sure hoped so!

I blew out a breath, suddenly impatient to learn just what my role was in all this. "I've told you everything I know. Now you tell me. Have you found any evidence, any emails or phone calls or other intelligence, linking Diane Roth or Oliver Austin to the Kissimmee murders?"

"No, nothing."

A huge boulder seemed to roll off my shoulder. I felt

nothing but relief that all my nasty suspicions were just that—unsubstantiated suspicions.

"So why am I here?"

"Before I explain that, would you tell us if Sergeant Roth has ever mentioned someone named Al Sorenson?"

"No."

"Dino D'Roco?"

"No."

"Hazra Ali?"

"No. Who are these guys?"

In response, Sinclair clicked a button on a remote. The blank screen at the far end of the conference room glowed, then came alive with the image of a smiling, middle-aged man waving from the cab of a dust-covered truck.

"Al Sorenson was a civilian contractor working at Bagram Air Base in Afghanistan. He ran the U.S. Materials Recovery and Reclamation Program until his vehicle hit an IED six months ago. Prior to that, we suspect he smuggled somewhere in the vicinity of five million dollars' worth of heroin back to the States in expended shell casings."

My momentary relief seeped away like water oozing through my fingers. I got all tense again as Sinclair brought up a tough-looking character in a gray uniform with scarlet tabs on each shoulder.

"Colonel Hazra Ali was deputy director of defense in Kunduz Province, northern Afghanistan. He died in the same blast that killed Sorenson. We now have hard proof he acted as Sorenson's go-between with the local warlords looking for a market for their opium crop."

"And Dino D'Roco?"

Sinclair brought up a police mug shot showing a curly-haired wise guy smirking at the camera.

"Dino was a small-time South Jersey thug until he started moving major shipments of heroin. Word on the street is he had a direct source in the person of his brother-in-law."

Sinclair clicked the remote again. The unshaven thirty-something in a black T-shirt looked vaguely familiar, but I couldn't place him.

"Who's that?"

"His brother-in-law. Oliver Austin."

Oooookay.

I took a closer look. Austin looked different without a ski mask pulled up to his forehead. And without the tire tracks! Handsome, in a brooding, George Clooney kind of way. I could sort of see why Diane went for him.

"We had Austin under surveillance for some time," Sinclair related grimly. "He was just a cog, a minor player who greased the wheel for the big guys. We gave him plenty of rope, hoping he, Sorenson, Ali, and Dino would lead us to those big guys."

"Both in Afghanistan and here in the U.S."

That came from Tom whatever his name was. The State Department rep. He scrubbed a hand across his stubbled chin, weariness in every line of his body.

"I'm sure you've heard opium production has increased exponentially since the U.S. busted up the Taliban regime, which kept the countryside in a stranglehold. Unfortunately, the present government hasn't been able to exert the same degree of control. With warlords once again reigning supreme in their private fiefdoms, the drug trade has exploded. Afghanistan now accounts for more than ninety percent of the world's opium trade and is in danger of becoming a total narco-state."

This was all making me extremely nervous. It didn't take Pen's two PhDs to connect the dots.

Multimillion-dollar international drug deals.

A cog in that disgusting wheel attempting to take out a woman he'd served with in Afghanistan.

The same woman who'd evidently lied about keeping in touch with him.

I clutched my mug of now-cold sludge with both hands. I was pretty sure I knew what was coming but asked anyway. "Why am I here? What do you want me to do?"

Sinclair's blue eyes lasered into me. "We want you to get close to Sergeant Roth. Very close. Find out what she knew about Austin's activities in Afghanistan."

Despite the ice in my veins I felt compelled to insert a caveat. "*If* she knew about them."

"If she knew about them," he echoed. "Become her new best friend. Get her to trust you. When it looks like she might open up to you, we'll fit you with a wire."

I squirmed in my chair, guilt running rampant. I knew

in my heart I'd done the right thing by contacting Sinclair but couldn't help feeling like a real scuzz for prying up the lid on this Pandora's box. Diane had already been through so much. Her and the kids. Now I could well be adding to their troubles. Some best friend!

CHAPTER TEN

ONCE I'd reluctantly agreed to Agent Sinclair's plan, he arranged for me to be granted a special security clearance. I then proceeded to learn more about the enormously profitable and extremely dangerous heroin trade than I'd *ever* wanted to know.

The big question, the one I was supposed to help them answer, was how much, if anything, Diane Roth knew about the operation in Afghanistan.

I'm not sure why Sinclair thought that I, a mere amateur, could squeeze more information out of her than he had. Both he and Comb-Over Guy had grilled her during their investigation into the shooting. What's more, the hot-dog analysts at HQ had picked through every line of her sworn statements, looking for holes or contradictions concerning her relationship with Oliver Austin. The only inconsistency they'd found until now was the one that had generated that eye flicker.

In her statement to both the El Paso PD and CID investigators, Diane claimed she hadn't responded to Austin's emails after he departed Afghanistan. But Sinclair and company found one in a screen of the thousands of communications generated at a computer center set up for the troops to keep in touch with family and friends.

"It doesn't contain anything incriminating," Blue Eyes admitted, sliding a copy across the conference table.

"No kidding," I commented after skimming the brief, single line indicating Diane had heard Austin might have to meet a medical eval board and was worried about him.

"But it does contradict Roth's statement that she hadn't kept in touch with Austin."

"It's only *one* email. Maybe she forgot it."

"Right. Like she forgot to tell you her in-laws had been murdered."

That shut me up. Blue Eyes gave me a moment to reflect before pushing out a tired sigh.

"Look, Lieutenant, I know your relationship with our local CID detachment isn't the best."

"What did Comb Over tell you?"

He bit back a smile. "Enough. Seems you have a tendency to color outside the lines."

I couldn't argue that. Mitch and I had both done some independent coloring after my lab got torched. We'd been taken to task for it, too.

"We need your help on this one, Lieutenant. It's big. Too big for you to talk about with anyone outside your direct chain of command. Or in it, for that matter. We'll brief your boss. Tell him what he needs to know. As far as this investigation goes, you talk only to me."

I departed CID headquarters with another cell phone in my purse. This one wasn't as gee-whiz as my DARPA toy, but it would link me via a secure line directly to Special Agent Sinclair or one of his people.

A fat, round moon shone through the bare tree branches as I steered the rental back toward D.C. It was past midnight, and I felt almost as wiped as the team who'd been working this issue night and day for months on end. I didn't envy them their task and couldn't repress an uneasy feeling at having been sucked into it.

This drug business is just plain ugly. As a Border Patrol agent, Mitch is right on the front lines of the counter-narcotics war. He doesn't talk about his job much. He doesn't have to. The daily papers and nightly news reports about the cartel violence in Mexico and potential for spillover to the States are scary enough.

Now I had a whole new dimension of the drug war to worry about. One that might or might not involve Diane Roth. I tried not to think about it as I checked into the hotel room Agent Sinclair had reserved for me just south of the D.C. Beltway and crashed.

I arranged a seven a.m. wake-up call before I dropped into total unconsciousness. The call came. I answered.

And promptly fell back asleep. I jerked awake again at 8:40 and let out a shriek. My meeting with Dr. J was set for ten.

I was out of the hotel and in the rental car in twenty minutes. Then, of course, I had to get lost twice on my way to DARPA headquarters. Not even the NAVSTAR navigational unit could aim me in the right direction.

"Turn left at the next intersection," the smarmy voice intoned.

I flipped on my directional signal, only to spot an orange-striped barrier blocking the side street.

"Turn left in fifty feet."

"I can't turn left."

"Turn left now."

"Hey! I can't!"

Gritting my teeth, I stopped to reset my current location and desired destination. I also pulled up the directions on my DARPA cell phone.

"Beam me home," I snarled at the two instruments.

They did. But not before I passed the Pentagon and circled Arlington National Cemetery twice. Finally I turned onto Fairfax Street and spotted the towering glass and sand-colored concrete building housing the headquarters of the Defense Advanced Research Projects Agency.

I had to get cleared by security to park in a visitor's space in the underground garage. Then cleared to pass through initial screening. Then cleared again for access to the inner lobby. I'm not complaining, mind you, since this building contains more brains per cubic inch than anywhere else on the planet—all devoted to improving the combat capability of U.S. troops.

They come from some of the most prestigious universities, research centers, and think tanks in the country. DARPA reaches out to them via what I call the visiting professor program. The idea is to keep the U.S. in the vanguard of technology by luring these incredibly innovative thinkers away from academia for four or five years, then handing them massive budgets and unlimited authority to explore new ideas.

I gotta say, it's working. I mean, where else would you find people determined to develop a ChemBot—a robot with an amorphous shape that'll let it squeeze under closed doors or through cracks in a wall to collect battlefield intelligence?

Then there's the Deep Bleeder Acoustic Coagulation Program being worked by the Tactical Biomedical Division. I don't understand all the parameters, but the project's stated goal is to field a portable, noninvasive, lightweight unit that would allow combat medics to identify and locate the full range of life-threatening bleeders.

That's the thing about DARPA. Every time I get to grousing about my little team and the occasionally absurd inventions we test, all it takes is a reminder of our mission to put things in perspective. Despite my occasional—okay, constant—complaining, that mission is the main reason I'm still in uniform. And speaking of uniforms . . .

Before hitting the elevators, I ducked into a ladies'

room in the lobby to make sure my unruly auburn mane was still more or less confined and the end of the thick braid clipped up. God forbid a single hair should touch my collar. The Air Force considers that a disaster right up there with nuclear proliferation and global warming.

I re-tucked my light blue blouse in the waistband of my slacks and straightened my uniform jacket. My black pumps and black leather shoulder bag got a quick buff with a damp paper towel. A swipe of Georgia peach lip gloss, a stroke or two of blush, and I was ready for Dr. J.

Please don't misinterpret these last-minute preparations. I certainly wasn't hoping to dazzle Dr. Jessup with my military spiffiness. As my supervisor, he knows that's pretty much a hit-and-miss proposition. I think it was more a country-cousin-comes-to-the-big-city syndrome. FST-3 and its two sister cadres don't often rub elbows with the big guys.

Being a lowly lieutenant plays into the equation, too. The handful of military assigned to DARPA are mostly senior officers who bring hard-won tactical or combat experience to the table. What I bring is chutzpah.

Hmmmmm. Maybe that's not such a bad attribute in a lieutenant. With that bracing thought in mind, I hitched my purse strap over my shoulder and breezed out of the ladies' room. Moments later, I breezed into Dr. J's outer office.

"Hi, Audra."

The trim brunette with a wireless receiver hooked over her left ear looked up and smiled. "Hi, Lieutenant."

Audra Hendricks is Dr. J's executive assistant. She's worked at DARPA for more than a decade, which is eight years and then some longer than either Dr. J or myself. She's a lynchpin in my continual efforts to improve communications with HQ.

Translation: she covers my ass. A lot!

"Dr. J's got someone in the office right now. As soon as they finish, I'll let him know you're here. Want some coffee while you wait?"

"Thanks."

I helped myself at the credenza across from Audra's desk and subtly pumped her for information.

"So the CID contacted the boss to arrange this visit, huh?"

"They did."

"Did the call weird him out?"

"No more than any of the calls he receives regarding you."

Was that good or bad? I was still trying to decide when the door to Dr. J's office opened and a distinguished-looking gentleman exited. Distinguished, that is, except for his total lack of eyebrows.

I tried not to stare. Honestly. When he glanced my way and nodded politely, I also made a heroic effort to refrain from asking if he'd ever worked with one of my team members. Oh, what the heck! Restraint was never one of my strong points.

"Dr. Reed?"

I'd guessed right. The gentleman paused on his way to the door. "Yes?"

"I'm Lieutenant Spade, OIC of Future Systems Test Cadre—Three. I believe you know one of my team members. Rocky, er, Brian Balboa."

Every vestige of color drained from his hairless face. He stumbled back a step, caught himself, and looked around wildly.

"He's not here, is he?"

"Dr. Balboa? No, I . . ."

"He'd better not be. The restraining order's still in force."

"Wait! I just wanted to ask you . . ."

Too late. He shot out the door as if the hounds of hell were about to take a bite out of his butt.

"Okay, Audra." I swung back to the executive assistant. "You *have* to clue me in. What's the deal with his eyebrows and Dr. Balboa's subsequent banishment to FST-Three?"

Smiling, she shook her head. "What happens at DARPA HQ stays at DARPA HQ. Hang on, I'll tell Dr. J you're here."

She buzzed the boss and waved me to his office door. I sucked in a deep breath, squared my shoulders, and walked in to find Dr. J had squared his, too. Or it could have been the padding in his checkered sport coat. Hard to tell, especially with the distraction of his fuddy-duddy bow tie. It was yellow today. With navy blue polka dots.

Brown checks, a yellow tie, and blue polka dots. That tells you almost as much about my boss as his jaw-dropping string of degrees.

"Hi, Dr. J."

"Hello, Samantha."

I could tell from his cool greeting that he was trying to strike an official note. Just his bad luck that supervising doesn't come any more naturally for him than being supervised does for me.

He cleared his throat, which set his tie bobbing, and waved me to a seat in front of his desk. "I'm very much hoping you'll shed some light on whatever you're up to with Special Agent Sinclair."

"I'd like to, sir. I really would. But . . . Well . . . Sinclair said he would drive up and brief you personally. In the meantime, he said to tell you that what he's asked me to do won't compromise FST-Three's operation or any of DARPA's ongoing programs."

Dr. J didn't roll his eyes, but I could tell he wanted to. I knew he was itching to remind me what happened the last time I mucked around in cop stuff. Our lab got torched, Mitch wound up with a tree branch through his shoulder, and my trusty, rusty old Bronco went up in flames.

On the plus side, I helped break up a stolen arms operation and received an AF Commendation Medal for my efforts. Which Dr. J himself presented, I might add.

I puffed out my chest a little, hoping to draw his attention to the blue-and-yellow ribbon, but he was too busy worrying about the dire possibility he might have to conduct another inquiry into lost or damaged government property. The last one took months and was not fun for anyone involved.

"From the little Agent Sinclair *did* tell me, I gather what he's asking you to do is connected to the shooting incident in El Paso. I hope you'll be careful, Samantha. Very careful."

Awwwww. I'd misjudged him. The doc was more worried about me than the lab or the possibility of another lengthy inquiry.

"I'll be careful, sir. I'm not real anxious to get shot at again."

"Good."

He shuffled through the papers on his desk and lifted one out. My team's final test report, I realized in his next breath.

"Now tell me about this NLOS system you tested. I'm intrigued by your supposition that it could contribute to the Urban Leader Tactical Response, Awareness, and Visualization Initiative."

With my head full of narco stuff, it took me a moment to make the transition to Techno Diva. I fumbled my way through atmospheric particles and solar-blind ultraviolet wavelengths, earning several extremely pained looks from Dr. J in the process. I must not have bungled the concept too badly, though, because he agreed with my assessment that the system warranted further testing.

"But please," he entreated. "Conduct all further tests under controlled conditions, following the proper protocols."

"Yes, sir."

Since I had a few hours until my four p.m. flight home, Dr. J took me to lunch in the executive dining room. He followed that unexpected treat with an update on some of the newer projects DARPA had out for bid. I managed to keep my eyes from bugging out at some of the wilder programs. The dollar figures attached to them were even more staggering.

I got back to El Paso too late to call Diane, so I left a message for her at work the following day. She returned my call that evening.

The moment I heard her voice I decided I didn't want a career as an undercover agent. I didn't like this sneaky feeling and had to work hard to keep my tone light while I fudged the reason for my call.

"Just thought I'd check," I told her. "Am I still on to play honorary aunt on Saturday?"

"You're still on, if you're up for it. I get off work at ten that morning, but have a ton of stuff to take care of."

"No problem. And Mitch said he'd treat Joey to some guy time. If he gets back from San Diego before the weekend, we can take both kids off your hands for a few hours."

"San Diego? Is that where he is? I called him yesterday to ask about Saturday and I got his answering machine. I didn't realize he was out of town."

I was surprised she had Mitch's unlisted home number. He gives it out very sparingly. With good reason. In his job, he makes as many enemies as he does friends. The bastard whose threats drove his wife and daughter away being a prime example of the former.

But then, Diane was a cop. She had access to all kinds of information.

"I'll call you Friday afternoon to confirm the details," I said casually. "Oh, and Diane?"

"Yes?"

"I've been thinking about Canyon Ranch. I may have overreacted a bit to their pricy services."

"A bit?"

"If I recall properly, you gagged over the price list, too."

"You're right, I did. But you said you've been thinking. Does that mean you want to give it another shot?"

"If you haven't already used the gift certificate."

"I haven't. What day is good for you?"

"I'm totally flexible."

I also had a mandate from higher headquarters authorizing me to take whatever time I needed to become best friends with this woman. I figured that could cover another day at the spa.

"When's your next day off?" I asked her.

"Sunday, but I don't know if Canyon Ranch is open then. I'll check and call you right back."

They were. Ten minutes later my weekend was completely booked with Roths, young and not-so-young.

The only glitch in our plans was that Mitch wouldn't fly in from San Diego until two on Saturday. I talked to him a couple times before that but didn't feel comfortable using an open phone line to pick his brain for any tidbits he might know about the Afghan heroin trade. We did coordinate our schedules, however.

Trish and I would make the one thirty showing of Tyler Taylor's new movie. Mitch would drive in from the airport and pick Joey up. We would then rendezvous for ice cream or whatever at a place of the kids' choosing.

To be sure I stuck to my end of the deal, I went online and purchased the theater tickets. I also Googled this TT character to see what had all the eight- and ten-year-olds so excited.

YOU would think watching YouTube videos pan across audiences of (a) rapturous, (b) goggle-eyed, or (c) hysterically giggling little girls bouncing up and down in their seats would have prepared me for Saturday afternoon. Not so.

I dressed in what I thought would be appropriate wear for the occasion. Ankle boots, jeans, a pale pink turtleneck, and a fleece vest done in swirls of hotter pink and cream. I left my hair down—hooray for weekends!—and slung my favorite Coach bag over my shoulder. Actually, it's my only Coach bag and getting worn from rough handling, but I'm hoping to eke another season out of it.

I could tell I'd broken the genetic code when Trish came dancing out of the Roths' apartment. She was in pink, too. Sneakers, jeans, jacket, even her hair ribbon. I waved to Diane, standing in the doorway with Joey and buckled my charge in.

The theater parking lot was jammed. My anxious passenger squirmed impatiently until I finally squeezed into a space between a pickup and a delivery truck. Praying my Sebring's bright, shiny paint job would remain un-dinged, I dug the tickets out of my purse and ushered my charge into the theater complex's cavernous lobby.

My forethought in purchasing tickets online got us past the throngs at the ticket booth but not those mobbing the refreshment stands and special kiosks set up to hawk the latest TT merchandise. Promising Trish a look at the merchandise later, I steered her past the kiosks and provisioned her with Skittles and diet Sprite. I fortified myself with a giant tub of popcorn, sure that could get me through any ordeal. The one that followed was worse, so much worse, than I'd anticipated.

I've taken nieces and nephews to movies before. Hard to get out of it, seeing as my various siblings have gifted the world with so many progeny. I've never had to suffer through anything like the crass commercialism in this flick, though.

There I sat, lost amid a sea of ecstatic youngsters and resigned parents, watching this idiot kid and friends break into song and dance while blatantly promoting everything from their funky socks to their scented hair gel.

No chance of getting by the kiosks in the lobby after that. Trish and I stood in line for a good half hour, but she left clutching a CD and a Tyler Taylor T-shirt. I left wishing fervently for a stiff shot of Grey Goose.

Sadly, there wasn't much chance of getting that when we joined up with Mitch and Joey. The kids had chosen a McDonald's close to their home as their number one choice for a rendezvous. I suppose I don't have to tell you Trish inserted the CD the moment we were buckled into the Sebring. Lucky me, I got to listen to Tyler Taylor all the way to Mickey D's.

I took Trish's hand, braced for the noise that would smack us in the face when we walked in. Pretty much every one of those nieces and nephews I mentioned had celebrated one birthday or another at a fast-food emporium. I knew from personal experience they were a busy, busy place come Saturday afternoon.

I was prepared for the wall-to-wall noise. I wasn't prepared, however, to spot Mitch and Diane sitting knee-to-knee at one of the tables. Or for the sight of her leaning into him as she angled her head and laughed up at him.

I came to a dead stop, still clutching Trish's hand.

"There's mommy. And Mr. Mitch!"

The girl tugged her hand free and skipped toward the table. I followed more slowly.

CHAPTER ELEVEN

OKAY, here's the thing. I'm not obsessively territorial. That time I walked in and found my ex with his jeans around his ankles and his face buried between our neighbor's 38Ds? I saw red, sure. But right on top of the first surge of shock and rage came disgust. With myself, not Charlie. I'd married a jerk who would cheat on me after only six months of semi-bliss. How dumb did that make me?

On that memorable occasion, I'd spun on my heel and walked. Out of the apartment, out of the marriage, out of the downward spiral that had been my life to that point. I certainly don't remember experiencing anything like the savage urge that got me by the throat as I approached Mitch and Diane. It took everything I had not to grab a fistful of a certain blonde's hair and rip it out by the roots.

"Hey, Samantha." Mitch smiled at me before giving the little girl who'd rushed into the circle of his arms an affectionate noogie. "How was the movie?"

When Trish launched in a passionate recount, I shifted my attention to the woman at Mitch's side. She was in snug jeans and a boxy, cable-knit sweater the color of ripe wheat. With her hair drawn back in a scrunchie, she looked casual and relaxed. Too casual. Too relaxed.

"I'm surprised to see you here, Diane. I thought you had a lot of business to take care of this afternoon."

"I did, but I got everything done early and decided to join you guys. You don't mind, do you?"

Her eyes were clear and direct, although I could swear I detected just a faint hint of challenge. She knew exactly how it must look to find her sitting shoulder to shoulder with Mitch, I realized. And she didn't care.

My lingering unease at agreeing to spy on a sister in arms evaporated at that moment.

"Why should I mind?" I returned coolly.

Shrugging out of my jacket, I joined them at the table. Trish ran off to find her brother in the jungle of plastic tubes and tunnels.

"How was San Diego?" I asked Mitch, too pissed to resume my role of Diane's best friend just yet.

"Busy. Informative." He scrubbed a hand across his chin. "Scary as hell. You want something to eat?"

"I pigged out on popcorn at the movies. I'll wait until later."

Later, when the two of us were alone. When I could give him a sanitized version of my quick trip to D.C. and ask him what he knew about heroin coming in from Southwest Asia.

My glance flicked back to Diane. She had her chin in her hand. A small smile played across her face as her youngest emerged from a blue plastic tube, squealing with delight. His sister popped out almost on top of him. Grabbing his hand, Trish hauled her brother toward a yellow cave.

"They're good kids," Mitch murmured. "You've done a heck of a job with them."

She had, I was forced to agree silently. Except . . .

Joey had spent almost half his young life with his grandparents. They'd shaped Trish, too, during her most formative, impressionistic, inquisitive young years. Much of the credit for their bright, bubbly personalities had to go to the Roths.

Deliberately, I changed the subject. "Are you still up for Canyon Ranch tomorrow?"

"I am! Mrs. Hall said she would watch the kids. The spa opens at ten on Sundays, so we've got the whole day. I can't wait."

Mitch slanted me a curious glance. "I thought all that decadence pricked your conscience. What made you change your mind?"

I did a big mental squirm. Feeding Diane a line over the phone was one thing. Lying to Mitch was another. Especially with his green-gold eyes looking into mine. Shrugging, I dropped my glance and snagged a French

157

fry from his tray. It was cold and soggy but gave me time to fumble a response.

"I thought it over."

That was true enough.

"My team and I have tested some far-out creams and lotions, but nothing in the commercial beauty product line. So I decided it wouldn't be a conflict of interest to use half of Diane's gift certificate."

Not so true.

A slight crease formed between Mitch's brows. We'd spent enough time together now that he understood what my team did. He understood as well the potential for civilian application of the items we tested. Ignoring the question in his eyes, I turned to Diane.

"Want me to pick you up tomorrow?"

"Why don't you drive to my place, but we'll take my car from there. I'm picking up a new Honda mini-van as soon as we leave here. I want to show it off."

"They couldn't repair the Tahoe?"

"They could, but I decided to trade it in." Her lips turned down in a grimace. "I knew I could never climb behind the wheel again without thinking about Ollie and that awful day."

I could understand that.

"We stopped by the dealership on the way here," Diane continued, brightening. "Mitch convinced the service manager to kick in a video system for the kids at no extra charge. They're installing it as we speak."

"They didn't take much convincing," he countered with a wry smile. "Your fame had preceded you. The service manager was only too happy to add to the package. They gave Diane a heck of a deal on both the trade-in and the new-car purchase price," he explained for my benefit.

I kept my mouth shut, but I couldn't help thinking Diane was really racking up the loot as a result of that "awful" day.

Okay, okay. I admit it. That snarky thought stemmed more from my aforementioned urge to rip out her hair by the roots than doubts about her involvement with Oliver Austin. Becoming her new best friend, I decided grimly, might be tougher than I'd anticipated.

I managed to bury my feelings during the rest of our sojourn at Mickey D's, but they surfaced again when we left. I had to stand there, a smile pasted on my face, while Diane and the kids piled into Mitch's pickup for the drive to the Honda dealership.

They'd wedged Joey's car seat into the cab's rear half seat. It took two to get him strapped in, Diane leaning over the front bench, Mitch angled into the narrow door opening. She was flushed and laughing when she plopped back down and waited for him to buckle Trish in.

The task accomplished, he came around the cab and reached out to zip my vest.

"The Honda dealership is on Lee Trevino Boulevard," he said when I had my chin buried in hot pink fleece. "Closer to my place than yours. How about I drop Diane and the kids off and meet you at the house?"

"You sure she won't need you to test drive her new

car? Maybe scrape the stickers off the window for her?"

I tried, really tried, to keep the acid out of my reply. Obviously not hard enough. Mitch hooked a brow before he answered.

"If she does, I'll call you."

Now I felt not only snarky, but stupid. We hadn't placed any boundaries on either our relationship or our friendship. Both were too new, and too casual. I covered my gaff with a shrug.

"Your place it is, then."

Nodding, he slipped his house key off the ring. "I'll be there shortly."

"Same alarm code?"

"Same code. I'll change it tonight."

As he did on a regular basis. A necessary precaution given his line of work.

FIFTEEN minutes later I cruised into the residential neighborhood where Mitch lives. The homes are mostly stucco with some brick and aluminum siding thrown in here and there. Chain-link fences divide the backyards, toys and bikes litter the grass stubble in front. Every second driveway sports a basketball backboard or soccer net.

Mitch had lived with his family in a three-bedroom ranch-style house until the divorce. When his wife moved out, she took their daughter and, at his insistence, everything that wasn't nailed down. That was three and a half years ago.

I pulled into the driveway, leaving room for Mitch to park beside the Sebring, and let myself in through the front door. The soft beep of the alarm system gave me ten seconds' warning. I knew Mitch had rigged both active and passive sensors. I punched in the code and took care of them both.

My footsteps echoed as I passed the empty living and dining rooms. Mitch had replaced only the bare minimum of furnishings when we first met. A man-sized leather recliner, a TV, an end table and lamp in the den. A table and two chairs for the kitchen eating area. A bed, nightstand, and lamp in the master suite. That was it.

He's since added a few extra touches. Most notably an overstuffed sofa long enough for me to stretch out with my head in his lap while we watch TV. Or for us to stretch out on together while we engage in more strenuous activities.

I wasn't in the mood for either at the moment. Tossing my jacket and purse on the chair, I kicked off my shoes and dropped onto the sofa. I did my best to talk myself out of my foul mood but was still working on it when Mitch's dusty pickup pulled into the driveway.

"Did you get Diane and the kids all set with their new minivan?" I asked when he appeared in the den.

He nodded and shrugged out of the suede bomber jacket I'd bought him for Christmas to replace the one speared by a tree branch. The jacket joined my fleece vest on the chair. Lifting my crossed ankles, he sat at one end of the couch with my feet in his lap. His fingers kneaded my sock-clad toes. His gaze locked with mine.

"You want to tell me what that was all about back at McDonald's?"

I started to bat my lashes and play dumb, but it's not really my style. Nor was confessing to a nasty little bout of jealousy. My voice gruff, I apologized.

"Sorry I sniped at you. Guess I was just, uh, surprised at how close you and Diane have become in such a short time."

"I wasn't referring to the sniping, although we can talk about that in a minute. I meant that bit about the spa." He massaged my toes, the crease back between his brows. "Why did you change your mind? What made you decide it wasn't a conflict of interest?"

I formulated a half dozen responses before giving him the truth. "I can't tell you."

His hand stilled. "Why not?"

"I made a quick, up-and-back trip to D.C. while you were in San Diego, Mitch."

"To DARPA?"

"Yes . . . and CID headquarters."

The crease cut deeper now. He stared at me for several moments, connecting the dots.

"This is about Diane and Austin, isn't it? Something that happened while they were in Afghanistan."

I tugged my foot free and sat up. Curling both legs

under me, I sorted through the sensitive information Blue Eyes had fed me and contrasted it with the information I'd dug up myself from online sources.

I knew I was on shaky ground here. Blue Eyes's instructions had been painfully specific. Tell no one, consult with no one, except him or his designated contact at the local CID detachment.

Yet this was Mitch. Aside from turning my insides to mush with one of his crooked smiles, he was the coolest-thinking man I knew. He also put his life on the line every time he strapped on his bulletproof vest and went to patrol another dangerous stretch of the U.S.-Mexico border.

I'd promised not to compromise the sensitive information Blue Eyes and company had force-fed me about the narco trade in Afghanistan. The other aspect of the Austin/Roth case, however, the one I'd become most directly involved in, had reached out to encompass this man sitting so close to me. I couldn't keep him ignorant of the potential for disaster.

Only later, much later, would I stop to wonder how much my visceral reaction to seeing Diane leaning against Mitch's shoulder played in my decision to share my suspicions. At this moment, I sincerely believed he needed at least a sense that the woman might not be exactly what she seemed.

"I can't tell you about Afghanistan, Mitch, but you can tell me something. Has Diane ever talked about her in-laws?"

The abrupt change in direction surprised him. "Not to me. You were the one who told me they'd tried to get custody of the kids."

But I hadn't told him about the murders. I hadn't had the chance since the cookout, when Diane's neighbor dropped that bombshell.

"The Roths were bludgeoned to death," I told Mitch. "In their own home."

His eyes narrowed. I could see the cop in him recalling details, sifting through them, sorting out facts.

"Diane told the police Austin rotated back to the States some months before she did," he said slowly. "When were the in-laws murdered?"

"Two weeks after Oliver Austin checked himself out of a VA hospital and disappeared."

"Well, hell!"

"Yeah, that was my reaction, too."

Especially after Agent Blue Eyes contradicted Diane's assertion Austin had been in the hospital at the time of the killings.

"I researched the murders online, Mitch. They were brutal. Two people beaten to death in what looked like a break-in gone bad. The newspaper reports were pretty gory, but I'm guessing the police released only selected details."

"I'm guessing you're right." His voice went flat and hard. "Where were the kids when it happened?"

"In school."

The hard edge didn't leave his tone. "So what are you thinking? That Diane had Austin take out her in-laws to end the custody battle? Or that he did it for love?"

I told you the man was one cool thinker. In fifteen seconds flat he'd zeroed in on the questions that had tortured me for hours before I finally picked up the phone to call Sinclair.

"I don't know what to think. I'm hoping to God neither she or Austin were in any way involved. But . . ."

I came up against the brick wall of Afghanistan and stopped. Once again Mitch connected the dots.

"But whatever took you to D.C. throws enough doubt on the issue that you changed your mind about spending a day at a spa with Diane. Or," he finished, a muscle ticking in the side of his jaw, "had it changed for you."

He was furious. Coldly, quietly furious. I couldn't blame him. I wasn't too thrilled with my role in all this, either.

"I'm not out to nail Diane, Mitch. I swear, I'm not. I'm just helping find the answer to some . . . some inconsistencies."

For a big man, he can sure move fast. I wasn't expecting his lunge. Or the iron grip on my upper arms.

"You little idiot. It's not Diane I'm worried about. She's a cop. She can take care of herself. You're the one breaking me out in a cold sweat."

Well! I was trying to decide whether that grim assertion should make me feel more gratified or insulted when Mitch gave me a small shake.

"Listen to me, Samantha. If the Roths' murders were

not the result of a burglary gone bad, we're talking a cold-blooded killer here."

Insulted. Definitely insulted.

"Right," I huffed. "The kind who opens fire at a crowded strip mall. I was there, remember? Right beside your tough, I'll-take-him-down cop."

He jerked back, bringing me with him, as my words hit home. We stared at each other for long moments while the ugly, unspoken accusation hung in the air between us.

"Let's get it out in the open," Mitch said finally, easing his grip. "Do you think . . . Does whoever you're working with think Diane crashed her vehicle into Austin with deliberate intent?"

"With deliberate intent? Yes. It was kill or be killed. The question now is, did she know it was Austin?"

I didn't want to believe Diane Roth knew or guessed the shooter's identity. I didn't want to think she'd made a desperate attempt to silence a man who might implicate her in two brutal murders and, possibly, drug smuggling on a staggering scale. Yet I couldn't get around that small, intentional lie about the hospital.

"My gut tells me she didn't know who the shooter was, Mitch. Everything happened so fast. Diane and I both acted instinctively. And I witnessed her reaction when the responding officer pulled up Austin's ski mask," I added, the scene all too vivid in my mind. "She was shocked out of her gourd."

Some of the tension cording the tendons in Mitch's neck eased. I translated that as relief that the woman we'd both spent hours with, the woman so obviously devoted to her children, hadn't deliberately made mush out of a possible coconspirator.

We settled back down on the sofa, closer together this time. With my back snuggled against Mitch's chest and my head tucked under his chin, I talked him through what I'd learned from my online research about the murders. That much was unclassified. That much I could share.

All the while, my conviction grew that he needed to know the rest. I wasn't the only one who could get chummy with Diane. This afternoon had made that painfully obvious.

Plus, Mitch would be a whole lot more effective at pulling information about Afghanistan from the woman than I would. They were both law enforcement types. He knew how her mind worked. He could get into it more easily than I could.

I decided to contact Blue Eyes after I left Mitch's place. The secure phone he'd given me was tucked in my purse. I itched to get to it as Mitch and I dissected the details of the Florida murders.

I wasn't surprised when he glommed on to money as a possible motive. I stretched my vow of silence enough to confirm that half the Roths' estate would be held in trust for the kids.

"That doesn't mean Diane couldn't borrow against the trust," Mitch countered. "Or break it, if one of the kids was in desperate need of, say, an expensive medical procedure."

"She's military. The kids' medical needs are covered."

"True."

He shifted, easing me a little to one side. Just enough for his five-o'clock bristles to scrape my temple as he laid a completely new wrinkle on me.

"Then you might want to have whoever you're working with check to see who gets guardianship of Diane's kids if anything happens to her."

CHAPTER TWELVE

GREAT! Just great!

As if I didn't have enough on my conscience after agreeing to spy on Diane and the nasty thoughts generated by the sight of her cozying up to my own personal Border Patrol agent. I felt guilty enough over my newly assumed role as a snitch. Now I had a whole new set of worries to contend with. Like who would assume guardianship of the kids if something happened to their mother. And whether that person, whoever it was, knew about the kids' inheritance.

I drove home Saturday night thinking about the unanswered questions. It was still on my mind Sunday morning while I got ready for my second excursion to Canyon Ranch. My hair went back in a scrunchie. My lips received a halfhearted swipe of gloss. I zipped myself into a marine blue jogging suit with white stripes worn over a white tank and thrust my feet into laceless sneakers.

With more than an hour to spare, I brewed a pot of coffee and toasted a bagel for breakfast. All the while this whole business of the Roths' estate kept churning around in my head.

Could Diane be the third and final target in a convoluted conspiracy to gain control of the Roths' wealth through their grandchildren?

It wouldn't be the first time something like that had happened. As I crunched down on my bagel, I dredged up the details of an article I'd read years ago in one of my favorite glamour mags. The subject of the piece was the downside of great wealth. Sure, the rich and famous jetted off to Monaco and yachted down to Acapulco. They also had to contend with minor inconveniences like stalkers and kidnappers.

As a historical perspective, the article cited the Osage Indians in Oklahoma and what happened to them after the discovery of oil on their tribal lands in the late 1800s. Maybe it was the early 1900s. Whenever.

The point is the massive amounts of black gold pumped from their lands made the Osage the wealthiest people on the planet at that time. The story even included a black-and-white photo of an Osage woman in a stovepipe hat being chauffeured around in a Rolls. Reportedly, her oil revenues gave her the modern equivalent of fifty thousand dollars a day in spending money!

I remember idling away a fun if totally fruitless ten

or fifteen minutes speculating on whether I could blow fifty grand a day. It would be a challenge, but I'm pretty sure I could do it. Filling an entire closet with Manolos and Jimmy Choos would certainly be a start.

But I digress. As the article pointed out, the Osages' huge wealth made them a target. Greedy whites began marrying into the tribe to get a share of oil headrights. Worse, so many Osage parents were murdered by outsiders attempting to gain guardianship of their children that the period became one of the darkest in Oklahoma history.

Cut to today. A single mom with no close relatives other than her children. The same kids who stand to inherit what could be a sizable fortune. Kids whose only parent had already been the target of one near-fatal attack.

Mitch's suggestion returned with blazing intensity. I couldn't get the idea behind it out of my head. Who besides Trish and Joey would benefit from Diane's death?

She must have executed a will and named a legal guardian for the children. The military ought to have access to that information. Maybe even have a copy on file. I was pretty sure she also had to designate someone to take care of the kids in the event she deployed again.

Not being a parent myself, I was a little hazy on that end of things. So I did what comes *very* unnaturally for me. I took my coffee and bagel over to my combination dining table/desk, powered up my laptop, and did a search of military rules and regulations.

Thirty seconds later I was staring at the title page to DOD Instruction 1342.19, "Family Care Plans."

"Oh, gawd!"

The groan came from deep inside, a visceral response to the prospect of plunging into the convoluted maze of DOD directives. I still break out in hives whenever I think about the reports and regulations I had to battle through after my lab got torched. With great trepidation, I opened the PDF file for 1342.19.

Monster relief! This sucker was only ten pages long. The last one I had to slog through ran to fifteen *volumes*! Happily, I crunched down on my bagel. A moment later, the crumbs turned to sawdust in my mouth.

"I should have known," I muttered glumly.

DOD Instruction 1342.19 referred me to DOD Directive 4001.1, then to 1200.7, then 1315.7, then . . .

See what I mean about that maze?

A zillion regulations later I had verified that a Family Care Plan was, in fact, required by military couples with children and by single military members solely responsible for a child or an adult dependent. DOD Civilians who were subject to deployment and had the same type of family responsibilities were also strongly encouraged to execute a plan.

In the plan, the responsible member was required to designate a short- and long-term caregiver, then arrange to provide that person with necessary legal documents and financial support in the form of allotments. The caregiver in turn had to sign a statement indicating they fully accepted the responsibility.

The only kicker I could see in Diane's case was that

service members had sixty days to notify their commander of a change in circumstance, like divorce or adoption or the death of a spouse or caregiver. They then had another ninety days to devise and submit a new care plan.

The Roths were murdered in November. We were now in mid-February. So Diane may not have completed a new plan. Still, it was worth a shot.

Gulping down the last of my bagel, I rooted around in my purse for the cell phone Special Agent Blue Eyes had issued me. I pressed a key and had him on the video screen mere moments later. He was in a suit and tie, with a church choir belting out a hymn in the background. Grimacing, I apologized.

"Sorry to get you out of Sunday morning service."

"Not a problem. What have you got?"

"Nothing yet. Just wanted to let you know that Sergeant Roth and I are spending today at a spa. I may have something later. In the meantime, how about checking her Family Care Plan to see who she's designated to look after her kids in place of her in-laws?"

"Why?"

"I was thinking . . . We don't know if Austin or his friends were involved in the attack on the Roths. We *do* know the kids are in line to inherit a portion of their grandparents' estate. We also know Austin tried to kill Diane Roth. Might not hurt to check out whoever's next in line to gain guardianship of the kids."

"I see where you're going with this. Only problem

is, the children don't benefit from their grandparents' will for a lot of years down the road."

"You know that. I know that. But Austin and friends might not have."

"True. I'll run a screen of her Care Plan. I'll also check out who she's designated as a secondary beneficiary on her SGLI."

Well, duh! Why hadn't I thought of Servicemembers' Group Life Insurance?

All uniformed members of the armed forces were automatically enrolled in the low-cost SGLI insurance program. Unless a troop opted out or chose to reduce the entitlement, he or she was covered up to a maximum of four hundred thousand dollars, with additional coverage for traumatic injury while on active duty.

I'd designated my mother as my primary beneficiary, my sisters and brothers as secondaries. Given our family's predilection for self-destruction, odds were half of them wouldn't live long enough to collect.

Most likely Diane had designated her kids as primary. But who after that? And was the secondary beneficiary the same individual as the caregiver on her Family Care Plan?

While I mulled over the possibilities, a glint of approval came into Sinclair's blue eyes.

"You put this whole string of possibilities involving the Roths' murder together, Lieutenant. I like the devious way your mind works."

"I'm not sure I should take that as a compliment."

"That's how it was intended. Ever think about becoming an agent with your Air Force's Office of Special Investigations?"

"Good Lord, no! I'm feeling guilty enough as it is about all this sneaking around Sergeant Roth. Besides, I . . . Uh . . . Didn't exactly put all this together on my own."

The admiring glint vanished. "Who have you been talking to?"

"A friend. Actually, he's more than a friend. Border Patrol Agent Jeff Mitchell. He helped bust a stolen arms operation and take down the creep who destroyed my lab some months ago. Comb-Ov . . . That is, Special Agent Hurst may have mentioned him when you and he drove out to the site."

"No, he didn't."

"Mitch is one of the good guys, Sinclair. More to the point, he's as familiar with the principals in the case you're working as I am."

I could tell by his tight-lipped expression he wasn't happy and rushed to explain.

"Mitch and I were meeting for dinner the night Austin opened fire. He arrived on the scene, like, minutes after it happened and met Diane that night. He even picked up her kids from day care while she and I waited to give our statements to the homicide detectives. He was at the cookout I mentioned, too, the one where Diane's neighbor told me about the Roths' murders."

I didn't bring up the McDonald's gig. That one was still stuck in my craw.

"And since Mitch is Border Patrol, he's on the front

line in the drug wars. I suspect he knows as much or more about the narco trade as any of you in D.C."

"It's possible," Blue Eyes conceded, "although from an entirely different perspective."

Perspective, my left foot! I started to ask when was the last time he got shot at. Or had to cut off all ties with his only child to keep her safe. Biting my tongue, I played nice instead.

"I'd like to fill Mitch in on what you told me. Clue him in to Austin's suspected activities in Afghanistan."

"Let me check him out first. I'll get back to you."

"Okay. In the meantime, I'll go get seaweed-wrapped with Diane Roth."

I drove to Diane's place through light, Sunday-morning traffic. The temperature was already close to sixty-five, with a high expected in the mid-seventies. That's one thing about El Paso in February. The nights are cold and starry but the days make up for it with plenty of sunshine.

Diane came out of the door looking bright and eager in a poppy-red jogging suit. I locked my car and we loaded into her new, silver-toned minivan.

"It doesn't give me the safe, heavy feel of the Tahoe," she confided as I buckled in, my nose twitching at its new-car smell. "But Trish and Joey love the swivel seats and play table. Guess I don't have to tell you they went nuts over the DVD player and game station Mitch had the dealer throw in. And look at this navigation system. I swear it could plot directions to the moon and back."

I kept my recent, frustrating experience with navigational systems to myself and duly admired the minivan's accoutrements.

I'm not sure whether it was the spring morning or the new car or anticipation of a day of sinful decadence, but Diane seemed more chatty during the drive out to Canyon Ranch than she normally was. Or maybe my guilty conscience had kicked in and I was listening harder for nuances in everything she said. Whatever the reason, I didn't contribute much to the conversation.

The one time I tried to steer it toward the subject of the kids' guardianship I was sidetracked by the jack-rabbit that hopped into the road right in front of the minivan. Those of you who hail from somewhere other than West Texas may not be familiar with the local breed. There's a saying out here that they come in three sizes—big, bigger, and stay the hell out of their way. I've also seen clay pots in the shape of the legendary jackalope, a cross between a rabbit and an antelope, complete with antlers and a saddle. I mention all this because the critter that jumped in front of the minivan was large enough to do a serious number on its shiny new grill.

Diane's lightning-fast reflexes saved the day—and the lop-eared jack. I twisted around and saw the dark sedan some distance behind us almost go off the road as it, too, dodged the creature. When I settled back in my seat and commented on her swift reaction, Diane grinned.

"You spend nine weeks in MP training at Fort Leonard Wood. Then you live and work and go out on patrol with a bunch of guys who still aren't sure women belong in uniform, much less on the business end of a grenade launcher. You learn to react fast in just about every situation."

That gave me the opening I'd been hoping for. I wasn't quick enough, however. Before I could ask about some of her experiences in Afghanistan and, oh, by the way, any heroin-related activity she might have witnessed, she preempted me.

"I've seen you in action, too. You move fast yourself, Lieutenant. They teach you that in wacko-invention-testing school?"

"I wish! Unfortunately, my team and I have learned pretty much on the job." I paused for a moment before taking the next step in my Best Buddy campaign. "We're off duty, Diane. Just two gals out to indulge in a day of sybaritic delights. Why don't you call me Samantha?"

"I can do that. So, Samantha, tell me about your ex-husband."

"Not much to tell. We met, we mated, we married in a moment of sheer insanity. Six months later we split."

"Why?"

"The usual reasons. Hot sex, followed by more hot sex. Just not with me."

"Bastard."

We proceeded to compare notes on the shortcomings

of our respective ex's until we turned onto the long, curving drive that led to Canyon Ranch.

JON was thrilled to see us again. His mauve coat flapping, he rushed into the reception area and folded Diane's hand in both of his.

"Sergeant Roth! Our very own heroine! I'm so glad you and the lieutenant decided to give us another try."

After he and I did the two-handed thing, he led us toward the double bronze doors.

"Susannah's *so* disappointed that she's booked with another client, but Erik and I will see you two are very well taken care of."

We pushed through the heavy doors into the airy, sky-lit forecourt and were immediately enveloped in a blend of subtle fragrances. Gardenia, I think, with just a hint of some exotic spice. Jon swept two embossed folders off the marble counter and passed them over as another mauve-robed attendant appeared from one of the treatment rooms. He was a blond, Nordic type, much bigger and considerably more muscular than his associate.

"Ah, here's Erik."

Jon made the introductions and presented us each with a folder before shooing us to our dressing rooms. For the second time in a little over a week, Diane and I occupied spacious cubicles extravagantly supplied with lotions, robes, slippers, and fluffy towels. Per Jon's instructions, I stripped and cloaked myself in freshly pressed linen.

Properly garbed, I took a moment to glance at the printed agenda. It began with a Monticelli body treatment—hot and cold stones to stimulate reflex points, improve lymphatic flow, and detoxify the entire body. A deep-tissue massage would follow, then an Inner-C bath—whatever that was!—a lemongrass wrap, body waxing, and the grand finale of a lip bloom. Designed, I read, to give me softer, shapelier, plumper lips and a more inviting smile.

I could live with plumper lips. Still, I had to remind myself that this was all in the line of duty before I emerged and found Jon, Erik, and Diane waiting. She'd clipped back her pale blond hair and belted the robe around her trim waist. She'd also used the brief wait to secure Erik as her personal attendant. That left me with Jon, who manfully hid his disappointment behind a smile and a flutter of his wrist.

"First stop, the body treatment room. Right this way, ladies."

Having hot and cold stones piled on your outstretched torso by industrious attendants doesn't lend itself to the kind of personal conversation I wanted to have with Diane. Ditto the deep-tissue massage, which I have to say brought out a surprisingly sadistic streak in Jon. His manicured fingers dug, kneaded, rolled, and dug again. I alternated between gasping in pain and groaning with pleasure.

I almost crawled to the Inner-C bath. That, thankfully, turned out to be a gentle wave pool infused with active marine ingredients and silk powder.

"This will restore equilibrium to your entire being," my personal sadist informed me.

After his pummeling, my entire being *needed* restoring. The wave pool helped, but it was the lemongrass wrap that truly corrupted me.

I stretched out on a table in another private treatment, this one draped with burnt orange and pale yellow batik. Jon whisked away my robe and left me only a skimpy, strategically placed towel before proceeding to revive my skin and my soul with a head-to-toe exfoliant. I was tingling with delight from that when he slathered on thick, silky lemongrass lotion.

"You need to lie here for twenty minutes while the moisture seeps into your skin," he instructed. "This wrap will help seal it in."

He swathed me from neck to ankles in thin, crinkly brown paper. Once I was properly mummified, he produced a set of wireless earphones and a remote.

"Classical music on station one, easy listening on two, soft rock and salsa on three and four."

No heavy metal or hip-hop for the patrons of Canyon Ranch, evidently. I was fiddling with the headset when I heard Erik's muffled voice issue the same twenty-minute warning in the treatment room next to mine.

I'd give her ten minutes to seep and seal, I decided. Then I'd casually saunter next door, brown paper and all. I used the interval to plot the perfect lead-in.

I would comment on how lucky we were that Mrs. Hall was available to babysit Trish and Joey today. I would follow that with a not-entirely-feigned concern over who would take care of the kids if Diane had to deploy again. From there I would segue into how tough it must have been for her to be separated from them so long in Afghanistan, especially with the hassle from her in-laws.

That was the plan, anyway. It fell apart when I attempted to sit up on the table. Still greased head to foot, I had to grab the edges to keep from sliding off. In my frantic groping, I almost missed the small, panicked grunt that came from the adjacent room.

When I finally got a robe around me and poked my head through the door, though, it was hard to miss the mauve-coated figure pinning Diane to the table with an elbow dug into her middle. Or the crushing force he was exerting on her windpipe with his other hand.

CHAPTER THIRTEEN

EVER try to take on a strangler while you're buttered up like a Thanksgiving turkey and wrapped in brown paper? Trust me—it is not easy!

After my shocked brain assimilated the fact that a wiry male in pale pink and rubber gloves had Diane in a stranglehold, I lunged. My creamed toes almost went out from under me on the slick tiles but I gained enough momentum to throw myself at the man.

He was so intent on his victim that my sudden attack caught him off guard and sent us both crashing into the counter that ran the length of the treatment room. Bottles and vials went flying as I screeched at the top of my lungs.

"Jon! Erik! Anyone!"

Wish I could tell you I employed some lethal guerilla tactic I learned in the military. Or one or two of the slick moves Mitch has taught me. Any offensive and defensive maneuvers I might have picked up, however, flew out of my head when Diane's attacker turned and came at me. My frantic brain recorded an image of eyes slitted with fury, lips drawn back in a snarl, and what looked like a purple birthmark on one side of a nasty jaw. Then I was pummeling the bastard with greasy fists while screaming my head off.

He got in some pummeling of his own. I took a sucker punch to the stomach, then a backhanded blow that sent me reeling into the table where Diane lay limp and gasping for breath.

The table gave me precious leverage. Hanging on to it for dear life with slippery fingers, I lashed out with my left foot. First time I ever wished I was wearing combat boots! Even without them, I put enough force behind my bare foot to crunch his groin.

Grunting, he doubled over. I locked my hands together, intending to bring them down on his exposed neck, but he recovered far faster than I'd anticipated and came up swinging. I dodged the blow aimed at my jaw by contorting backward over the table again. Another blow was on the way when the door to the treatment room crashed back on its hinges.

"Lieutenant! What . . . ?"

That's all poor Jon got out before the attacker spun around. Cursing, he slammed a rubber-gloved fist into the spa attendant's face. Jon went down like a swatted fly. The attacker leaped over him and ran.

I was still bent backward over the table. Uncontorting, I fought for purchase on the tiles with my lemongrassed toes. By the time I'd gotten my feet under me and gave chase, there was no sign of the attacker in the center court.

Panting, I thrust through the bronze doors, rushed past the startled receptionist, and hit the front entrance. I burst out onto the steps just as a dark sedan tore around the corner of the building. Spitting up a plume of dust and gravel, it sped down the drive. I wasn't 100 percent certain, but it sure looked like the same dark sedan I'd spotted in the rearview mirror on the drive to the spa! I squinted through the plume of dust but all I caught were the first two digits of the license plate.

"Dammit!"

Gathering the pale pink robe around my papered limbs, I rushed back inside.

"Call nine-one-one," I instructed the gaping receptionist. "Tell them one of your customers has been assaulted."

More than one, actually. Jon had taken a hit, too, but I was in too much of a hurry to correct myself. When I reentered the treatment area, I found a half dozen people crowding the entrance to Diane's room. I pushed past customers with heads wrapped in towels and faces wearing varying shades of shock to find Erik on his knees, holding a towel to the nose of a dazed and profusely bleeding Jon.

Diane was sitting up on the table. Supported by red-haired Susannah and another attendant, she held a trembling hand to her throat. Her eyes were wide, the pupils dilated and stark with terror.

"You okay?" I asked over the pumping of my heart.

"I'll . . . live." The words came on a hoarse croak. "What about . . . you?"

I would feel the elbow hit and shoulder punch later. Right now the adrenaline was still firing on all cylinders.

"No serious damage done."

She swiped her tongue along her lips and swallowed with obvious pain. "Is he . . . ?"

"He's gone. He must have run out a back door while I was running for the front. Bastard had a car waiting for him there. He spun around the corner and took off. Hopefully," I said with a glance at Susannah, "the spa's security cameras got a good shot of him and his vehicle."

"Someone go call our security service," she said to the small crowd still hovering at the door. "And get this woman a cup of tea with honey!"

My gaze shot back to Diane. "Who was he?"

"I never . . . saw him . . . before."

"Did he say anything?"

She dragged her tongue across her lips again and let her shoulders slump. When she raised her head, I don't think I've ever seen such raw misery in anyone's eyes before.

"I have to talk . . . to that investigator from . . . CID headquarters."

* * *

GUESS I don't need to tell you the El Paso police weren't real happy with the victim's decision to clam up until Special Agent Sinclair could hop a plane and boogie on out to West Texas.

The responding officers recorded the facts of the assault. When they tried to pry a possible motive out of Diane, though, she shook her head and reiterated her desire to speak with CID. That earned her a real nasty look and a ride to the station in the rear cage of the black-and-white to talk to the detective assigned to the case.

I scrambled into my blue exercise suit and followed in the minivan. The new car smell got my nose twitching again but I had started to feel the ache in my stomach so I couldn't fully appreciate the car's delicious aroma. As soon as we were beyond the red rock canyon walls, I flipped up my cell phone and dialed Mitch.

"What's up, Samantha?"

He sounded terse and distracted. I suspected the near-hysterical torrent of Spanish I could hear in the background had something to do with his distraction.

"You out on patrol?"

"I was. Right now I'm shepherding five coyotes to the detention center."

Coyotes, I knew, was Border Patrol slang for drug runners.

"Where are you?" he wanted to know.

"On my way to EPPD's northeast station."

"Why?" His voice sharpened. "What happened?"

"Someone tried to strangle Diane at the spa."

"Holy Christ!"

"She's all right," I added quickly, "but the attacker got away. She says she doesn't know who he was. She won't say more, though, without the presence of a certain CID agent."

"Guy by the name of Sinclair?"

"Yes."

"He called me a little while ago. Wasn't happy that I'd butted into his investigation and . . . Yo! Hombre! Yeah, you! *Siéntese!*"

"You've got your hands full. I'll let you go."

"Wait! If I know you, Samantha, you probably beat off Diane's attacker."

"I did. Would have taken the creep down, too, if not for the blasted lemongrass."

"Huh?"

"I'll explain later. Call me when you can."

THE El Paso Police Department's northeast region borders the Fort Bliss military reservation all the way up to the New Mexico border. As a consequence, its detectives have established a strong working relationship with the CID detachment on post. A fact Detective Mark Ruiz pounded home once Diane and I had been escorted inside the pink adobe command center.

A lean, intense type with curly black hair and babe-magnet chin whiskers, Ruiz did serious justice to a pair of snug jeans and a rumpled white Oxford shirt open at the neck. A loosened red tie hung crookedly below that strong, square chin.

"I contacted the CID duty officer." His serious brown eyes raked over my slick face and uncombed, towel-tossed red mane before lingering on the vicious finger marks ringing Diane's throat. "They just called to say Special Agent Hurst is on his way to the station."

"Oh, Lord."

My low mutter didn't escape unnoticed. The detective shot me a narrow-eyed look. "You got a problem with that, Lieutenant?"

I didn't think this was the time to reveal that Comb Over and I had something of a history, none of it good, and shook my head.

"Wait here," he instructed me. "Sergeant Roth, come with me and we'll take some photographs of your injuries."

Sunday must be a relatively low crime day in the 'burbs. I took a seat in the waiting room opposite a father and son who'd come to report a stolen bicycle. The only other occupant was a middle-aged blonde in leopard-print spandex tights and a ratty, faux fur jacket. Gripping a paper cup of coffee in hands tipped with bloodred nails, she glared at me, at the man and his son, at the desk sergeant, and everyone who passed by.

Special Agent Andrew Hurst received an especially nasty glare when he stalked into the station. From me, not Faux-Fur Gal. In justification, I should point out that the look I gave him was a direct response to the one he zinged at me. He must have been doing some Sunday-morning yard work when the CID duty officer contacted him. At least I *hoped* that was the reason for the leafy green twig decorating the sparse strands plastered across his otherwise bald head.

"Where's Sergeant Roth?"

"Detective Ruiz is digitizing her bruises."

Nodding, he turned to the desk sergeant and showed his credentials. "I'm Special Agent Hurst, CID. Is there an interview room where I can speak with the lieutenant privately while we wait for Detective Ruiz?"

"Second door on the right."

"Thanks."

We relocated to the small, cheerless room done in institutional beige.

"Sinclair is catching the next flight out of D.C.," Hurst informed me. "He expects to be here by six our time. Now what's this all about?"

I told him what I knew, which wasn't much. Then we sat and pretended to be polite until Detective Ruiz escorted Diane into the room. The impatience stamped on the detective's sexy, whisker-shadowed face suggested their session had included more questioning than mere photography, with less-than-desirable results.

Ruiz and Hurst did the man thing, crunching each other's fingers, while Diane slid into a seat beside me. She looked awful. The finger marks ringing her throat had already started to purple. Much worse was the lost, almost desperate look in her eyes.

"I'm tempted to charge her with obstructing a law enforcement investigation," Babe Magnet bit out to Hurst. "The sergeant knows more than she's telling us."

They both cut Diane swift glances. It took a visible effort on her part, but she lifted her chin and returned their look. "I'll tell you everything I can after I talk to Special Agent Sinclair."

"Then you'll keep your butt planted in that chair until he gets here." Ruiz turned back to Hurst. "I'm assuming the assault is related to the shooting incident and vehicular homicide Sergeant Roth was involved in a couple weeks ago. Anything you want to fill me in on before I interview the lieutenant?"

"Sorry, Mark. I'm just an assist on this one. Special Agent Sinclair will have to coordinate release of information to civilian authorities."

"Right." His jaw worked. Ruiz didn't appear real happy about the way the military community had closed ranks. "I've contacted the homicide detective working that case. He wants in on this interview, too. In the meantime, we've got our patrols on the lookout for the dark sedan Lieutenant Spade saw leaving the spa. Sergeant Roth, wait here. Lieutenant, come with me."

I accompanied him to another interview room and related my perspective of the incident at the spa. He pumped me on the shooting, too, before leaning back in his chair and lacing his hands across his middle.

"Interesting that you were present both times Sergeant Roth was attacked. Are you a great believer in coincidence, Lieutenant?"

"Well . . ."

"I'm not." Head cocked, he studied me thoughtfully. "You ever think maybe you were the target, not her?"

Okay, I'm not ashamed to admit it. My eyes popped and my mouth sagged open in surprise. I must have looked like a hooked trout as my cheeks puffed in and out.

"I . . . Uh . . ."

Took a moment for my brains to unscramble. When they did, I dumped the list of disgruntled inventors that had instantly materialized inside my head.

"I wasn't the one in Oliver Austin's sights the day of the shooting. He took aim at Diane. And the guy at the spa . . ." I shook my head. "He couldn't have mistaken her for me. We don't look anything alike."

"It was just a thought." He shoved to his feet. "I'm going to run the description you and Sergeant Roth provided through the National Crime Information Center database, see if I get a hit on that birthmark. If I do, I'll need you to make a positive ID. You can leave then."

"If you don't mind, I'll stick around until Sinclair shows."

"Why should I mind?" The sarcasm was so thick it almost bounced off the walls. "I'm only the investigating officer. You military types are running this show."

Properly put in my place, I sat and twiddled my thumbs for a while. Went to the bathroom. Dug my zipper clutch out of my jacket pocket and treated myself to a full-octane Coke to soothe my frazzled nerves. After that, I altered a few minor details of the composite the sketch artist had pulled together and hit the vending machines again for some stale peanut M&Ms.

Then I sat with Comb Over and a very subdued Diane in the waiting room for several loooong hours. When Special Agent Blue Eyes walked into the command center I heaved a huge sigh of relief. Too soon, it turned out, because another familiar law enforcement type walked in with him.

Tall, wavy-haired, and good-looking in a brooding, Al Pacino kind of way, FBI Agent Paul Donati swept the waiting area with hooded eyes. He nodded to Hurst and gave Diane a thorough once-over before turning to me.

"Hello, Samantha. Sinclair warned me you were involved in this."

I shot Blue Eyes a look of reproach. "Wish he'd warned me that *you* were."

I'd butted heads with Paul Donati during the hunt for the rogue agent who torched my lab, and, oh by the way, arranged two gruesome murders. Almost four, if you count Mitch and me. For some reason the FBI seems to think it's their job to take down that kind of slime. They don't particularly appreciate outsiders messing around in their investigation.

Kind of like Mark Ruiz. The detective made little effort to disguise his impatience after the newcomers duly identified themselves.

"How about we get this show on the road? Lieutenant Spade, I'll have to ask you to wait here while we interview Sergeant Roth."

I started to protest that I'd been cleared for this but Sinclair sent me a silent warning and drew Ruiz aside. After their little chat, I ended up with Andy Hurst in an airless observation room, listening and watching through a one-way mirror while Diane confessed to a horrifying tale of murder and blackmail.

"It started in Afghanistan," she related slowly, painfully, "over a couple of beers. I'd been out on perimeter patrol earlier that day. We took some sniper fire; one of our team got hit. I was pretty shaken. The whole squad was. Then, when I got back to base and checked my email, I found one from my lawyer. My in-laws had filed another petition in family court to get custody of my kids, using my extended absence as justification."

She put her elbows on the interview table and dropped her head in her hands. When she lifted it again, her face was dead white.

"I was pissed when I met Oliver Austin that night. Really pissed."

"Oliver Austin?" Ruiz echoed. "The shooter you took down here in El Paso?"

She nodded. "I don't remember exactly what I said. I swear I don't. All I know is that Ollie let me rant on and on. Then he . . . Then he asked me how much it would be worth to get my in-laws off my back."

None of the three men in the interview room moved so much as a muscle. I wasn't that controlled. Feeling sick, I locked my arms around my waist.

"I laughed," Diane whispered. "Just looked at him and laughed."

"You didn't name a price?" Sinclair asked when she broke off. Eyes haunted, she shook her head.

"No! I swear! I thought he was kidding until I saw the look in his eyes. Speculation, I guess you would call it. Or calculation."

My fingers gouged deeper into my waist. I had to remind myself to breathe as Diane continued.

"Some other guys came up to us and Ollie dropped the subject. He never brought it up again. Ever. It scared me, though. That conversation. That look in his eyes. That's when I decided to let things cool between us."

She was begging them to believe her, but they had their cop faces on. All three of them. They kept silent, forcing her to continue.

"Ollie was due to rotate back to the States in a few weeks. I asked my squad leader to detail me to a forward firebase until he left. You can check with Sergeant Barry Houseman. He'll verify that."

"We will."

Swallowing, she continued. "Ollie emailed me after his departure. I didn't answer."

"You sure about that?"

Confusion blanked her face. "I'm su . . . Oh, wait. I may have replied once. When he wrote that he'd been hospitalized. I remember now I sent a short email wishing him a quick recovery. Then . . . Then . . ."

The sick feeling in my stomach intensified. I knew what was coming, but it still hit hard.

"Then," she forced out, "I got word my in-laws had been murdered. I requested an emergency curtailment and flew straight to Florida. It was awful. Horrible."

"Did you talk to the police? Tell them about Austin?"

"I started to. But . . ."

"But?" Sinclair prompted.

"I called the VA hospital. They told me Ollie was still there so I knew he couldn't have committed the murders."

Blue Eyes didn't buy it. His voice as sharp as a serrated blade, he laid into her. "It didn't occur to you Austin might have tapped one of the contacts he'd made smuggling heroin to do the Florida job?"

"I didn't *know* Ollie was smuggling dope. I . . . I had my suspicions. He always had some kind of deal in the works. But I never knew any details. I swear! Until this morning."

She dragged her tongue over her lips, looking as sick as I felt.

"That man . . . The one who attacked me. He said Ollie arranged the hit on my in-laws through someone named Dean or Dino or something."

A wolfish glint jumped into Sinclair's eyes. "Dino D'Roco?"

"I think that was it. He said . . . He said this Dean or Dino had paid him fifty grand to kill the Roths."

Her hand went to her throat. Feathering shaky fingers around the vicious red marks, she hovered on the verge of breaking down completely.

"He told me this was payback," she whispered raggedly. "First, for dumping Ollie and trying to cut him out of the Roth deal. Then for taking him out of the picture completely."

CHAPTER FOURTEEN

THE interview continued for hours. Ruiz, Sinclair, and Paul Donati took turns pumping Diane for more detail. About Oliver Austin's activities in Afghanistan. About her legal battle with her in-laws. The shooting incident. The attack at the spa. They raked through the information again and again, until my initial disgust over Diane's failure to tell the Florida police about Austin gave way to reluctant sympathy.

She looked so devastated by it all, and so exhausted. Toward the end of the interview, her shoulders sagged and she had to use both hands to raise a paper cup of water to her lips. When they finally finished with her, she could barely drag herself out of the chair.

I felt almost as wiped just from listening to the in-quisition. That's my only excuse for fumbling the face-to-face with Diane when we emerged from our respective rooms at the same time. Sinclair, Hurst, and Ruiz went down the hall toward the front entrance. Donati headed for the men's room. That left me momentarily alone with Diane, who glanced in the dimly lit observation booth.

"You were watching? Listening?"

When I nodded, a puzzled frown creased her forehead. "But I thought . . . That is, the first time I spoke to Special Agent Sinclair . . . He told me anything I said was extremely sensitive and close hold. He stressed that I should speak only with him. That's why I insisted on waiting till he got here."

"I know. He told me the same thing."

Her frown deepened. "Then why . . . ?"

I realized I'd slipped up when she staggered back a step.

"Oh, my God! You're working with them, aren't you? With Sinclair and Hurst?"

"Not working *with* them, exactly. Just . . ."

Her weariness evaporated, replaced by a rush of anger. "Just *what*, Lieutenant?"

"I called Sinclair, okay? After Ms. Hall told me about your in-laws being murdered. I kept thinking there had to be a connection."

"I can't believe this." Breathing hard, she bunched her hands in the pockets of her red exercise jacket. "I trusted you. I thought we were friends."

I came within a hair of blurting out that I'd had a hard time generating real palsy feelings after watching her cuddle up to Mitch. I managed to bite that back but did add a pointed reminder.

"Whatever else you may think of my contacting Sinclair and company, it paid off when I went with you to the spa this morning."

"Right," she ground out, her jaw tight. "I'm sure I'll express the appropriate gratitude ... once I get past being pissed."

She spun on her heel and stalked down the hall. I followed, feeling almost as angry and resentful. The throbbing ache in my stomach didn't help matters. Nor did the nagging guilt that I *might* have been somewhat motivated by jealousy when I launched my Best Buddy campaign.

That uncomfortable feeling was still with me when we departed the station. Dusk had given way to the endless, star-studded night skies I've grown used to out here in West Texas. The temperature had dropped accordingly, so I zipped up my jacket and tucked my chin inside the stand-up collar.

Diane rode with Hurst and Ruiz, who wanted to scope out her neighborhood and apartment. The plan was to add extra patrols to keep both her and the kids under surveillance until they nabbed the man who'd attacked her and admitted to murdering the Roths.

Donati and Sinclair headed downtown to the FBI's regional offices. Blue Eyes didn't say so but I got the impression that Diane's revelations had given him the added ammunition he needed to lean on this D'Roco character in hopes he would finger the big guys.

That left me to drive Diane's new minivan back to her house. While I sped through the star-spangled night, I tried to work up a righteous indignation to counter her anger at my duplicity.

I *had* screeched the warning that had her dodging a bullet. *And* fought off a strangler intent on exacting revenge. *And* tried to suggest that Oliver Austin had, in fact, orchestrated her in-laws' brutal murders.

She'd known that, or at least suspected it. Yet she hadn't so much as mentioned him to the police. So where did she get off railing at me for helping the authorities get to the bottom of this vicious morass? And why the heck did I still feel so guilty about my role in all this!

I didn't admit the truth until I'd pulled into Diane's assigned parking space outside her apartment. I sat there for a while, letting my gaze roam the four-apartment unit while I tried to come to grips with an ugly realization.

I admired the heck out of Diane's courage in going after what we all thought at the time was a mass shooter. I respected her obvious and unstinting love for her kids. Admiration and respect aside, though, I didn't like the woman. Period. End of story.

It wasn't just the play she'd made for Mitch, although I still had a hard time getting past that. It was a bunch of little things. Playing to the media. Accepting all those freebies. Using her heroine status to negotiate a cut-rate deal on a new minivan. None of them big deals by themselves. Collectively, they added up to someone I wouldn't choose as a friend.

Except I had. Deliberately and with malice afore-thought. So what kind of person did that make me?

Geesh! Nothing like coming full circle! Wracked with guilt again, I knocked on Diane's door. I caught a shadow of movement behind the drawn drapes and knew either Ruiz or Hurst was checking me out before Diane opened the door.

"Here's your car key."

"Thanks."

Her expression was as unfriendly as the clipped re-sponse. I should have left it at that. Guilt—and my fatal tendency to butt in when everyone tells me to butt out—prompted an offer that surprised me almost as much as it did her.

"I know it has to worry you that the spa guy is still on the loose. If you like, I could take Trish and Joey to my place tonight."

"I called Mrs. Hall. She's going to keep them un-til . . ." She had to stop and draw a breath. "Until it's safe."

"Okay. Well . . ."

"Yeah. Well."

She shut the door and I made my way to the convertible I'd parked at the curb when we'd left for the spa this morning. I should have driven straight home. That's cer-tainly what I planned to do. What I *would've* done if that darned "until it's safe" hadn't buzzed around inside my head.

As I drove out of the apartment complex I kept think-ing of Joey and prissy little Miss Trish. They'd already lost their grandparents in a brutal double homicide. Almost lost their mother, too. Not once, but twice. Those attempts had failed but might prompt another approach. What better way to get back at Diane than through her kids?

That sickening thought had me fumbling in my purse for the cell phone Sinclair had given me. He answered on the second ring.

"What's up, Lieutenant?"

"Detective Ruiz said they were going to keep Diane under surveillance. What about her children?"

"She's left them with their designated caregiver. She says they'll be safe there."

"Designated?" I echoed.

"Right. After your call this morning, I checked her Family Care Plan. Roth submitted a revised plan two weeks ago, designating Annette Hall as both short- and long-term caregiver for the kids. By the way," he added on a note of fierce satisfaction, "we got a hit on the perp from the spa. His name's Vincent Capelli. He flew into El Paso yesterday and rented a midnight blue sedan from Hertz."

"Flew in from where?"

"Newark, New Jersey. Capelli is one of D'Roco's boys. Reportedly does a lot of Dino's dirty work for him, although the FBI hasn't been able to pin anything on him. Maybe this time."

I didn't like that "maybe" any more than "until it's safe." This was all getting too darn scary. So scary I found myself changing direction. Moments later I dimmed my headlights and flashed my ID to the guards manning Fort Bliss's twenty-four-hour Cassidy Gate.

You'd think a sprawling, frontier-era military post would be relatively quiet at nine p.m. on a cool, crisp Sunday evening. You'd think wrong. Fort Bliss is a major training center, remember? I pulled over to let a convoy on its way out to the range for a night-fire exercise rumble past. A little way farther on I slowed for a troop of joggers in Army-drab sweatsuits banded with orange reflective tape. They huffed past with the sergeant at the rear calling out a cadence that lifted my brows. I've heard some pretty inventive rhyming during my months at Fort Bliss. The lines that followed this "I-don't-know-but-I've-been-told" sequence, however, presented a new and *very* imaginative play on the word "duty"!

A reluctant grin tugged at my lips as I drove past Officers' Row, with its tile-roofed adobe quarters built circa 1893, then turned onto Pershing Road. No lights showed in the windows of the building housing FST-3's offices. I punched in the security code at the side entrance to let myself in.

Ever notice how spooky empty office buildings can be? Especially thirties-era buildings with floors that creak and outdated HVAC systems that tend to burp and hiss. I didn't waste time. Just hurried down a hall lit by the reddish glow of emergency exit signs and flipped on the lights in my office. I lingered there only long enough to grab the NLOS system.

I tucked the carton under my arm and retraced my steps. When I opened the exit door, I came face-to-face with a terrifying, two-headed apparition. My already shredded nerves unraveled completely. Shrieking, I hurled the carton containing the NLOS system at its upper head.

"Hey!" The creature ducked and flung up an arm to fend off the missile. "Hold your fire, Geardo Goddess!"

Gulping, I forced my heart out of my throat and back down to my chest. I recognized O'Reilly now, but it's going to take a *long* time to erase the startling image of his crinkly orange hair haloing his head like an alien's space helmet and the lens of his glasses glowing demonic red in the reflected light of the exit sign.

I also belatedly recognized the holographic face imprinted on his gray sweatshirt. I should. Anatoly Karpov, who Dennis considers the greatest chess player of all time, adorns his chest often enough.

"What the heck are you doing here, Dennis?"

"A World Chess Federation player in Indonesia challenged me to a match. We're connecting at five a.m. our time, but my home computer has a slow connection so I came for the laptop I left at the office."

That was O'Reilly. Why bother with sleep when you could push bishops and rooks and pawns around a computer screen all night?

"I saw your car in the parking lot," he said, knuckling his glasses back into position. "What are *you* doing here so late on a Sunday night?"

"Retrieving some equipment."

I edged past him to reclaim the carton. Luckily, it had landed in the bushes beside the door.

Dennis leaned over to peer at the carton. "Isn't that the NLOS system?"

"It is."

His eyes went wide behind the red-tinted lenses. "Are you taking it for another test drive?"

"Sort of."

"With no preestablished test parameters? No instrumentation to record the results?" A diabolical smile added to his already ghoulish appearance. "Rocky's gonna have a cow."

"Probably. Gotta go."

"Wait! Let me get my laptop and I'll come with you."

He darted inside and was out again with a computer case slung over his shoulder before I'd reached my parked car. Halfheartedly, I tried to discourage him.

"I'm not sure you want to tag along, Dennis. There's more going on right now than you know."

"So tell me," he said as he plunked himself down in the passenger seat.

I put the carton in the rear seat and slid behind the wheel. To tell the truth, I wasn't all that averse to having some company. The attack at the spa this morning had left me a little jumpy.

I pulled out of the parking lot and had just started to explain my intent when my cell phone pinged. The number on the LCD display was as familiar as my own. More familiar, come to think of it. Who calls their own number, anyway?

"Hi, Mitch. Did you get your band of drug runners taken care of?"

"I did. Where are you?"

"On post. I had to stop by my office."

"How's Diane?"

"Still pretty shaken when I left her place a little while ago."

That caught Dennis's attention. He twisted in his seat and sent me a questioning glance. I held up a finger, promising an explanation as soon as I got off the phone.

"When are you heading home?" Mitch asked. "I want to swing by your place and get the skinny on what went down this morning."

"Actually, I'm not heading home. I'm going back to Diane's apartment complex."

"Why?"

"I'm worried about the kids. She's left them with Mrs. Hall until all this is over but I . . . uh . . ."

What? Hoped to soothe my guilty conscience by babysitting the babysitter?

"Just wanted to check on them," I finished.

A short but speaking silence ensued. Mitch knew me too well.

"What are you up to, Samantha?"

"Nothing."

Much. I fended off further probes with a hurried promise to call him later.

Flipping the phone shut, I told my unintended accomplice what was going down. The incident at the spa filled him with shock and righteous anger on Diane's behalf. Those emotions diminished noticeably, however, when I hinted that the attacker might be a professional hit man responsible for at least two brutal murders . . . and that he was still on the loose.

Nervously, O'Reilly tugged at the neck of his gray sweatshirt. "You're, er, not suggesting we use the NLOS system to hunt this killer, are you?"

"Lord, no! All I want to do is provide a second line of defense for Diane's kids so this guy can't get to her through them. Once we deploy the sensors, we'll just sit nice and safe in the car. If anything looks even remotely suspicious, we'll call in the cavalry."

Completely unaware of the inadequacy of that blithe assurance, I pulled into a Starbucks to fortify us with grande nonfat caramel cappuccinos before heading north again.

OUR coffees were steaming up the windshield when we cruised past Diane's four-apartment unit. We didn't encounter a patrol car or note any parked vans that might contain a surveillance team. Not that either of us was all that familiar with police surveillance procedures. For all we knew, they could have set up passive sensors and be monitoring her apartment from a vehicle parked two blocks away.

Which is exactly what I intended to do with the NLOS sensors. As soon as I verified Annette Hall's address.

"You're riding to the rescue and you don't know which direction to head?" Dennis asked with a touch of his usual acid.

"Diane told me she lives in the neighborhood."

But where? There had to be at least a hundred or more units in the complex. Pulling over, I flipped up my phone again. Instead of going high-tech via Google and MapQuest, I went the good, old-fashioned route and dialed information.

"Got it!"

Darkness had descended with a vengeance now. We had to squint to see the numbers on the buildings but finally found Hall's unit. It was a good half mile away from Diane's, although I noted a big, grassy playground she and the kids could cut through to shorten the distance. I drove past Hall's building and parked halfway down the block. Twisting around to reach into the box, I extracted the tubular goggles and egg carton containing the sensors.

"You take six and scatter them in front of her apartment," I instructed Dennis. "I'll go around back. Don't forget to activate the switches."

"I won't." He pocketed the shiny round sensors. "Any suggestions what I'm supposed to do if I get mistaken for a peeping Tom or burglar?"

"Don't worry. I've got connections with the EPPD. If you get pinched by the cops, I'll bail you out."

Not particularly reassured, Dennis exited the Sebring. I did the same. The pockets of my jogging suit sagged from the weight of the sensors as I made my way back down the block and around to the rear of the unit.

As I had that fateful day at the shopping center, I

switched on the sensors and planted them in strategic spots. My intent was to cover the gate leading to Hall's fenced backyard from all possible angles. I placed one sensor on a stone ledge, two atop trash cans, another on a covered parking support beam, The last one I wedged in the Y of a tree branch.

All my sensors deployed, I circled back around to check Dennis's progress. I spotted him throwing nervous glances over his shoulder as he scurried back to the Sebring. Pudgy, geekish O'Reilly is not exactly hero material, as he himself made clear when he dropped into the passenger seat, huffing from his sprint.

"I'm having serious doubts about this, Samantha."

So was I, but I switched on the goggles and slid them in position atop my nose with the slit at eye level. My world narrowed instantly to a tiny slice of dark, starry night. I knew what to expect this time, though, and braced for the barrage.

It hit with a wallop. All of a sudden dozens of flickering, green-tinged images came zinging at me from all directions. Reflected by moonlight, they weren't as blinding as those reflected by sunlight. Still, my head jerked back and my eyeballs seemed to spin in their sockets.

Took a few moments, but I finally managed to focus on one image and exclude the others. I turned my head to the left inch by cautious inch. Slowly, so slowly, I sifted through the images until I located the rear of Annette Hall's apartment. The sensor I'd wedged in the tree reflected a clear view of her back door.

I had the hang of it now and was able to inch my head around enough to focus on the front without making myself dizzy and nauseous. Wish I could say the same for Dennis!

I had to take a break after about a half an hour and asked him to spell me. Talk about your basic disasters!

The goggles wouldn't fit over his glasses. Dennis couldn't see squat without the Coke-bottle lenses, however, so we angled the glasses on atop the goggles. Neither one of us considered the magnification effect that would have on the imagery. I got a good sense of it, though, when he let out a mind-shattering screech.

"Get away from me!" Flailing both arms, he battled an invisible foe. "Get away!"

I ducked one of his fists but the other plowed into the cup he'd set on the console. The dregs of his nonfat caramel cappuccino splattered all over me as I yanked off both glasses and goggles.

"It's okay! Dennis, it's okay."

He stopped flailing and blinked owlishly. "This dude who attacked you and Sergeant Roth," he said after a dazed moment. "Did you leave him with a world-class bruise on his chin?"

"Bruise? No, but he's got . . . Oh, my God!"

Cappuccino dripping from my cheeks and chin, I whipped around and crammed on the goggles.

"Where is he? Where did you see him?"

"In the back alleyway."

By sheer force of will I managed to get the whirling

images under control and focused on the carport behind Annette Hall's apartment.

And there he was! Capelli, or whatever the hell his name was. Bigger than life.

The birthmark looked like a small purple squash blossom as he rounded the hood of a dark sedan and made for the gate to her fenced backyard.

CHAPTER FIFTEEN

I still couldn't believe it! Capelli, right in front of my eyes.

"Dennis, call nine-one-one!"

"I don't have my phone with me," he squawked. "Where's yours?"

My heart hammering, I kept my head as still as possible to maintain focus and jammed my hand in my purse. I could tell from the shape of the instrument I pulled out it wasn't my high-tech DARPA jobbie but the instrument Agent Blue Eyes had issued.

"I'll make the call."

Waving off O'Reilly's attempt to grab the phone, I flipped up the lid and pressed the button that gave me a direct connection to Sinclair. The second he answered I shouted into the phone.

"He's here! Capelli! I've got him in view as we speak."

"Here *where*?"

"Casing the apartment of the caregiver for Diane's kids! He's at the back gate, for God's sake! You need to alert . . . Oh, no!"

"What?" Sinclair yelled in my ear. "What's happening?"

"The gate wasn't locked! He's in the backyard. Get someone here fast!"

All I could think of were the Roths bludgeoned to death in their own home. Tearing off the goggles, I wrenched on the door handle.

"Samantha!" Dennis lunged across the console to grab my sleeve. "Wait for the cops!"

"I can't. This bastard's already killed two people."

I shook Dennis off and leaped out of the Sebring. Cursing my decision to park a half block away and rely on the NLOS system, I charged toward Hall's unit. My blood thundered so loudly in my ears I didn't hear Dennis behind me until I rounded the end of her unit and skidded to a stop.

They were both there, visible through the open gate. Capelli and Annette Hall. Clearly illuminated in the light streaming through the back door. Stunned, I saw that the arm Capelli had hooked around the woman circled her waist, not her throat. And she was shaking a finger at him.

Shaking a finger, for God's sake! Like an elderly aunt or grandmother chiding a recalcitrant child. I was still rooted to the pavement in shock when Dennis huffed up beside me.

"Is that him? Is that the guy?"

"It's him."

"So wh . . . ?" Planting his hands on his knees, he bent over to suck air into his lungs. "So what's the deal?" he wheezed. "Do those two know each other?"

"Apparently," I forced out, still in shock.

Like bricks banging down on my head, the pieces fell into place. Hall moving to El Paso just a few weeks after Diane. Striking up a casual acquaintance at the playground. Letting drop how lonely she'd been since her husband's death. Spouting that line about how Joey and Trish filled the hole in her heart. Encouraging Diane to designate her short- *and* long-term caregiver, with full legal rights over the kids.

Although Sinclair hadn't mentioned it, I would bet everything I owned Diane had designated Hall as secondary beneficiary on her Servicemembers' Group Life Insurance as well. A nice, four-hundred-thousand-dollar bundle on top of what the kids might inherit from the Roths.

It was all planned, I realized with sickening certainty. Right from the start. If not by Oliver Austin, then by one of his sleazoid pals. And now, I saw with a leap of sheer fury, one of the players in this murderous game was about to get away.

Annette had handed something to Capelli. A key? A folded piece of paper? I couldn't tell at this distance.

He slid whatever it was in his pocket and turned to leave. The gate swung shut behind him. Hall went inside, closing the apartment door behind her.

"Where the hell are the cops," Dennis said in desperation as Capelli approached the sedan.

On their way . . . I hoped! I knew O'Reilly and I couldn't face the bastard down, alone and unarmed. But I could sure as heck delay him a few precious seconds by borrowing a page from Diane's tactics.

"C'mon."

Grabbing my still-huffing software guru by the arm, I hauled him back to the Sebring but thrust him aside before he could reach for the door.

"Stay here."

"Why? What are you . . . ? Samantha, wait!"

Ignoring his panicky yelp, I jumped into the driver's seat. The Sebring growled to life just as headlights speared through the night a half block away.

I doused my own car's lights and let my foot hover over the gas pedal. The headlights grew brighter. When the sedan nosed out of the alleyway behind Hall's apartment unit, I stomped down on the gas. Tires squealing, the convertible leaped forward. I had only a few seconds to mourn the sacrifice of my shiny new car before it broadsided the sedan.

I caught a glimpse of Capelli's face snarling at me above the pale balloon of an airbag but didn't stick around to wait while he fought his way free of it. Leaving the Sebring's front end embedded in the sedan's now-concave driver's side door, I bailed and sprinted back to Dennis.

He was goose-eyed and mourning his own loss. "My laptop . . . My chess database . . ."

"Forget the damn database and run!"

We didn't have to run far. Only a few yards before an unmarked patrol car screeched around a corner. Ruiz leaped out from behind the wheel, Comb Over from the passenger seat. A frantic Diane ejected from the rear.

"Trish and Joey! Annette! Are they okay?"

"I think so. Capelli didn't go inside, just talked to Annette at the back door."

"*Talked* to her?"

"Where is he?" Ruiz demanded while a shell-shocked Diane tried to process what I'd just told her.

I hooked a thumb over my shoulder. Ruiz spotted the cojoined vehicles and whipped out his semi.

"Stay back and let us handle this."

They got no argument from me. I was more than happy to let them take it from here.

Much as I dislike Special Agent Hurst, I have to say he moves fast. Within seconds he and Ruiz were on Capelli like junkyard dogs.

Diane wasn't interested in the drama unfolding down the block. Still trying to grasp the implications of what I'd told her, she grabbed my elbow and dragged me around.

"What do you mean, this guy talked to Annette?"

"Just what I said. They know each other, Diane. Annette and Capelli. He looped an arm around her waist. She shook a finger at him."

"What?"

"She chastised him like an irate mom. It looked like she was scolding him for something. Not finishing the job Dino sent him to do is my guess."

"Oh, my God!"

Whatever her other failings, Diane doesn't lack smarts. She made the leap instantly.

"They're after the Roths' money! All of them. Ollie. His so-called associates. Annette." Fury blazed from every pore of her body. "That *bitch*!"

She spun on her heel and shot toward Hall's apartment building. I panted after her, my breath rasping in my throat. I'm embarrassed to admit it, but I sounded almost as out of shape as O'Reilly.

We dodged Ruiz and Hurst, who had Capelli out of the sedan and spread-eagle on the pavement. Ignoring Comb Over's startled shout, I chased Diane down the alleyway to the Hall's gate. Diane flew through it and wrenched on the back door. When it didn't give, she hammered it with both fists.

"Annette!" The door rattled under her assault. "Annette, it's me!"

I caught up with her in mid-pound. "Be careful. You don't know what she's . . ."

That's all I got out before the door was yanked open. A startled Annette gaped from Diane to me and back again.

"What in the world . . . ?"

That's all *she* got out before the savagely furious mother hauled back and let fly. Her fist plowed into Hall's face with a resounding crunch. The woman crumpled and would have hit the floor if I hadn't caught her. Despite her slender silhouette, she packed some weight! I sagged to my knees with Hall dragging me the rest of the way down.

Shoving past us both, Diane ran inside. I heard her footsteps pound through the kitchen, into the living room, up the stairs. By the time I wiggled out from under Hall and made it to the foot of the stairs, Diane had already started back down.

"They're asleep. I left them until . . . Until . . ."

Her voice hitched as the fury that had driven her leached away. In its place came great, wracking sobs.

"Oh, God. Oh, God, oh, God, oh God!"

Sinking like a lead weight, she dropped onto one of the stairs and buried her face in her hands.

"My babies," she cried, as broken and desolate as I'd ever heard her. "I can't believe I trusted that woman with my babies."

I hunkered down and wrapped an arm around her. Sobbing, she turned her face into my shoulder.

AS with the other incidents involving Diane, this one took a long time to wrap. In the process we collected quite a crowd of interested parties.

Sinclair and Paul Donati both rushed to the scene. As did a whole battalion of additional cops, investigators, special agents, a fire department emergency response team, EMTs, and bunches of curious neighbors. I'd contacted Mitch, who was on his way as well, and in a somewhat belated call to arms, Dennis had put out an urgent summons to the rest of FST-3.

While we waited for reinforcements, O'Reilly and I huddled on Annette Hall's front stoop beside a thoroughly drained Diane. She'd left the front door open in case the kids woke up. She was praying they would sleep right through the wailing sirens and flashing lights. I hoped so, too, and didn't envy her the job of telling two bewildered children that the babysitter they'd grown so close to was apparently involved in— or at least had knowledge of—their grandparents' brutal deaths.

Annette Hall now sat handcuffed in the back of a squad car. I could see her pinched face peering through the rear window while the EMTs worked on Capelli. Evidently the side air bag had saved his upper torso from serious injury but the Sebring's bumper had crunched his lower leg. Can't say I felt much remorse over that.

A screech of truck tires heralded Sergeant Cassidy's arrival. Noel must have been doing his usual three- or four-hour nightly workout because his hooded black sweatshirt clung to his muscled-up chest in damp patches. Eyeballing the investigators surrounding my Sebring, he jogged up the sidewalk.

"You okay, Lieutenant?"

"I'm fine."

His gaze swept over O'Reilly, noted Diane's slumped shoulders, and locked on me again.

"Dennis said something about the NLOS system and

you crashing your car. Please tell me you didn't try to drive wearing those goggles."

"I didn't try to drive wearing those goggles." But that reminded me. "We need to retrieve the sensors, Dennis."

O'Reilly, Cassidy, and I garnered some odd looks from the assorted investigators as we collected the little round disks. I tucked them back in their egg carton, thinking that I owed the inventor one heck of an endorsement. I'd have to come up with some creative prose explaining this second, unauthorized deployment of the NLOS system before I could forward said endorsement to Dr J.

Rocky didn't help on that end when he and Pen arrived. Pen was in her usual layers of natural fibers topped by a down-filled vest that added beaucoup inches to her stocky figure. Rocky was in a world-class snit.

As Dennis had predicted, our test engineer was *not* a happy camper. Once he and Pen had assured themselves their team leader was still in one piece, Rocky expressed his feelings with some force.

"You can't keep conducting these unscripted, uncoordinated field tests, Samantha."

It wasn't a test, but I could see he was in no mood to split hairs. I hung my head and tried for penitent.

"I know."

"This is twice now you deployed the NLOS system without establishing proper parameters. Worse, we weren't set up to capture the data transmitted by the sensors. It's lost. Completely lost."

"I know."

"Then you also know you most likely invalidated the tests we conducted out at the site."

I could only play sorry for so long.

"Tests you declared inconclusive at best," I countered.

"That's beside the point. They were conducted under controlled conditions with trained observers to record the results."

"True, but did they bag an admitted murderer? Or his suspected accomplice?"

That deep-sixed the remainder of Rocky's tirade. Lips thinned, he palmed his thin, sandy hair. "You'd better stress those results to Dr. J when you explain tonight to him."

"Trust me, I will!"

Mitch pulled up at that point and provided a welcome distraction. Extremely welcome! Especially since his first move was to tug me into his arms to make sure I still had all my working parts.

His second move was to ask about Trish and Joey. He didn't try to hide his relief when I assured him they'd slept through the whole incident.

Diane came in a distant third. I didn't gloat. I swear I didn't. But I'm only human. So I enjoyed that reaffirmation of his priorities almost as much as his hard, fast kiss? Get over it.

CHAPTER SIXTEEN

WE were the lead story on all the early morning news shows. Diane. Her in-laws. Capelli. Oliver Austin. Annette Hall, whose real name turned out to be Holly LaRosa.

She really was a widow, only she'd lost her husband to a hit by a rival mob, not a heart attack as she'd told Diane. After that traumatic event, Dino D'Roco had taken her under his protective wing. In return Holly performed various small tasks for him. Like smuggling dope. And moving to El Paso to worm her way into Trish and Joey's hearts in hopes of cashing in on their inheritance. For that I sincerely hoped she spent a long, long time in a prison jumpsuit.

I earned some mention in the media coverage, although it was pretty much as a footnote. The big story—

again—was Diane. I caught the coverage when she appeared stony-eyed at an early morning news conference and announced that her kids had sacrificed enough for her military career.

"I'm requesting a humanitarian discharge," she told the reporters thrusting mikes in her face. "I can't put my children through another traumatic separation."

As I crunched down on my usual breakfast bagel, I felt a tug of genuine sympathy for the woman. She'd made the right decision. No question about that. Trish and Joey *had* endured more than any kids should have to. Yet I couldn't help remembering Diane's emphatic assertion that she was damned good at her job.

I suspected she would be toting a gun again soon, this time as a civilian cop. A suspicion Mark Ruiz confirmed when he contacted me at work early Monday morning to tell me I wouldn't need to drive up to the regional command center. Diane had positively ID'ed Capelli as the man who attacked her at the spa and bragged about killing the Roths.

"She's one tough cookie," Ruiz said with a hint of reluctant admiration. "She walked right up to Capelli, looked him square in the eye, and told him he was going down. I was impressed. So was my captain. He told her to come see him once our investigation and the one in Florida are wrapped up."

I didn't remind him Special Agent Sinclair also had an ongoing investigation. Whether Diane, Capelli, and LaRosa would play in that one, too, had yet to be determined.

My role, however, was definitely over. A point I stressed to Dr. J when I called him. His bow tie was chartreuse this morning. That odd, yellowish shade my mother calls baby-puke green. Not particularly flattering, especially when topped by a wounded expression that told me I was a tad late getting to him. Again!

"Good morning, Samantha."

"'Morning, sir. I guess you heard."

"About your activities last night? Yes, I did. Special Agent Sinclair contacted me. He said you and another member of FST-Three . . ."

He paused for me to fill in the name. I kept silent. If there was any negative fallout from last night I wanted it to fall on me, not Dennis.

". . . captured a suspected murderer," the boss finished.

I nodded, waiting for the NLOS ax to fall. It wasn't long in coming.

"I also understand you deployed the system we discussed when you were here at headquarters."

"Yes, sir."

His hurt expression eased as a hint of excitement crept into his eyes. "So it worked?"

"Like a charm."

"Send me your report as soon as possible. I want to see the data analysis."

"Well, uh . . ." Deep breath here. "We didn't record any data."

"What? Why not?"

"The decision to deploy the system was sort of spur

of the moment. I didn't have time to set up test proto-cols."

The spark of excitement fizzled. His face crumpled. I had to carry that look of disappointment with me for the rest of the day.

It hung over me like a dark cloud when I met Mitch for dinner after work. A hearty blue cheese and mush-room burger with a side order of cheese fries dissipated some of the cloud. Mitch blew the rest of it away when we adjourned to my apartment.

"Diane and the kids have had a rough time of it," he commented as we caught the tail end of a news update on the sensational case. "It'll probably get rougher before it's all over. I feel sorry for them."

"Mmmm."

They say confession is good for the soul. It didn't win me any Brownie points with my boss earlier but I figured I might as well make a clean breast of things.

"I got the impression Diane feels something for you, too."

"Yeah," he said with a careless shrug. "I picked up that vibe."

"Kind of ticked me off."

"I picked up on that, too."

"So?"

"So why don't we turn off the TV?" His smile slow and lazy, he worked the buttons on my ABU shirt. "Let me show you why you had nothing to be ticked about."

"Sounds like a plan to me."

Grinning, I hit the remote and went into his arms.

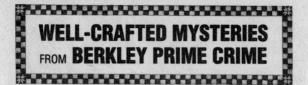